Emancipated

The Lady and Her Pentagon

Ericka Reynolds

(Tara Devi Ma)

Lady and Her Pentagon Series:

1. Enslaved

2. Enlightened

3. Emancipated

Also by Ericka Reynolds (Tara Devi Ma)

The Adventures of Cleo and Sophie - Trip to the Moon

E-book ISBN: 979-8-218-63334-9

Paperback ISBN: 979-8-218-63333-2

Dedication

This book is dedicated to all those who have freed themselves from their mental plantations and to those who are mapping out their escape plans!

My mission is to support others who are seeking freedom from their metal plantations. I do this by assisting you reconnect with your soul and obtain inner peace. If you should discover while reading this book that you are ready to emancipate yourself, feel free to connect with me!

taradevima.com

Emancipated

Prologue

What happens to the runaway slave that's still a slave but yet free? Constantly looking over your back thinking at any moment you can be captured. What if they made it as far north as they could? Free and clear, believing with great certainty they would never be found only to look up one day and see the master's overseer. They finally have a life of their own, finally feeling free. Do they surrender? Do they return to the plantation vowing never to escape again surrendering to the misconception that this is their fate? Do they keep trying to escape until they are eventually free? And how hard do they fight the next time they are captured to regain their freedom? And for those who did escape, started new lives, and were never captured, were they really ever free of the fear of being captured? How horrible to live the life of a "free person" who is never free to relax into their new existence that is until the Emancipation Proclamation and even then, would you trust that to protect you?

Fast forward to the 21st Century. How many of us walk away from something we know does not serve us but yet never feel comfortable in the new world we've created? Just like those escaped slaves, we feel like impostors always looking over our shoulders waiting to be taken back to the misery we fought to leave behind.

1

Back at Shawshank

I work at the Pentagon and everyone I know is aware of this fact. I think perhaps I didn't really get it. I have had a pretty indifferent opinion about it all these years - just a place where I work in support of our nation's defense. While the nation's defense is a big deal the rest was well, whatever. I never thought about what it represents to people and couldn't relate to those who took pictures of it as we would take off or land at Reagan Airport. I'd grin and bear it if I had to take my family inside while they were visiting. Afterall who wants to go to their job on their day off. But as I was driving back from California last week, I saw our new F-35s being tested at Nellis Air Force Base and well they were some sexy looking things flying around. Yeah, I know the issues and yeah, they cost a lot but damn they just looked nice! A feeling of pride hit me and I thought, "I support this!"

Seeing those F-35s made me re-think for a moment. I finally stopped contemplating my great escape when I saw those F-35s or maybe they were F-22s flying near Nellis Air Force Base (okay I've got a ways to go before I'm that deep in caring about our fleets). Whichever fighter they were, those things were the shit! Watching them flying around with speed and force was something sexy to see. And it was at this moment that I began to see what others see when they see the Pentagon. They see our military and these aircraft are a huge part of it. They see defense, promise, and hope. They also see a lot of whack stuff on television that inflates their view of this place but hell, just seeing these flying machines put a big smile on my face.

It took two decades for me to become impressed with where I work. The Pentagon. I looked at moving to the D.C. area and taking a new position with the Air Force as a way to escape the shitty life I was living in Oklahoma. To me it was just another Air Force job. Little did I know of the things that went on inside the "Beltway" and the politics that surround Shawshank. The more I learned of the place the less I liked it. But seeing those fighters changed my perspective. Somehow in my hatred of all things political about the place, I forgot I am there to support the mission. And let's be honest it's pretty cool to say I work for the Department of Defense at the Pentagon.

For 21 years I've worked for the Air Force and never had a thought as to what the general population must think but seeing those fighting machines flying in that beautiful Vegas sky made me say, "wow"! Whenever I'd note where I worked over the last year, I'd get these looks of fascination and wonder. These looks came from those in my group meditations and the numerous agents, executives, directors, and producers I was blessed to connect with for my writing career. While returning to the building was not something I was excited about I believe now God had me return to feel this level of pride while working there again.

So, I was pumped up enough and able to get the girls and I back here safely. But in my heart, I know this excitement and vanity will quickly fade so I must stay open to the true purpose for why I have returned.

This return is going to be okay.

Facebook, June 24, 2016

My lil role model ❤. Cleo's peacefulness is the same whether she is near the ocean or in a park that backs up to a neighborhood in Arlington. It's all about her joy of watching these squirrels. Location is a non-issue.

Now everyone knows I'm back in the DMV. Our last day in beautiful Santa Monica seems like a decade ago and it was only seven days prior.

It's funny how I once thought of Crystal City as a city ten years ago when I came here for a house hunting trip and now it feels like the suburbs compared to D.C. proper and Los Angeles. It's funny what you experience and how it changes your perception of things. I actually love coming to this park but I hate Pentagon City Mall. It's the closest mall to the district and it's always crowded during spring break with tourists. And I don't bother to come here during the summer, well only by necessity which this kind of is as I want Thai food and I need to go to the pet store. So after hanging with the girls at the park I am in errand mode and my life lesson from Cleo is fading.

The homeless population has really increased in Crystal city over the last decade. Last night I gave my last seven dollars to a homeless woman. Today I'm watching a homeless man cuss out a police officer. During my year in Santa Monica, I saw so many homeless people and yet they felt familiar, part of the community. Here they feel out of place though I am sure it's because I've not really seen them other than in D.C. In either case, from coast to coast they are all out of place as they should be provided shelter and support.

2

New Plan

I'm walking from my apartment to the Pentagon. As I slowly make my way there it hits me really hard. I can't believe I'm back here. I'm literally back in the same apartment building I first lived in when I moved here from Oklahoma. Sure, I picked the place again because it is in walking distance and I don't plan to be here long so why buy a place or even look to rent a home but I have to believe there is something subconscious in this decision. Perhaps it's because I was assigned to the same office I started in nine years ago. For the couple of days we've been back it's almost like an episode from the *Twilight Zone*. Walking my dogs in the same park, crossing Army Navy Drive and walking through the tunnel to get to Shawshank. Hearing the cars overhead as commuters rush into D.C. to start their workdays. Not one thing has changed since I innocently arrived here years ago except the innocence is long gone and I see this place and many things about myself so much clearer now.

Maybe this is my reset. God put me right back where I started so I can make different choices now. Of course! I know more now. I am more enlightened. I will approach things differently this time. This time I will write. I will go to those writing events around town. I will do what I was supposed to do then. This time I won't get comfortable. This time I understand my mission and will stay on track. I will do as Mona suggested and look at this as an extended business trip just like my fellowship was this past year.

In a way yes, this is like the *Twilight Zone.* I have been sent back to the past to create the future I deserve to have. Many of my spirit guides and angels came through during my last session with Mona. Even my grandmother came through to tell me all would be well so it has to be. I just need to do my part.

I make my way to the end of the tunnel. There it is. Shawshank. I only came here twice over the last year and both times felt rather unceremonious and distant. By the second trip I just knew California was going to be my new home so to walk in here felt like nothing. Now, I take a deep breath and another and one more before I allow myself to walk across the parking lot.

Looking around at the cars parked, the people getting dropped off at the slug line, the buses roaring in to the drop off the masses, I am still. I realize I just pumped myself up with the whole *Twilight Zone* thing but I don't want this – not one part of it. Okay Ava, keep moving. Today you are just out-processing from your old office. The real test will be on Monday when you come back to start your new position. You have the entire weekend to pray and meditate for more answers and strength. For now, remember the plan. Stay but don't get comfortable, minimize all your stuff that you just got out of storage so you'll be ready for an easy move back but understand that to get back you must ***write your way back.*** Finish the novel. It will be a huge success and it will take you home.

As I show my badge, I feel a lump in my throat. I keep moving and swipe into the building. I take a moment to really see everyone. Afterall that is why I am back, right? To be an investigative reporter.

No one is happy. Not one smile on anyone's face. Miserable people who could have very well been in great spirits right before they entered this building. Perhaps today is their anniversary or today is the last day before they start a two-week vacation but you would never know it by looking at these stoic faces. My first observation is the darkness. There is a dark heavy energy here that I didn't know how to describe before. How could there not be a dark energy? This place is a bureaucratic nightmare that plans and executes wars. There's death and destruction that is infused in the walls of this place. No one here is working on anything happy and light. Sure, someone may have an assignment to work on an off-site morale building Wingman Day event and someone might be assigned to support Military Family Appreciation Month but all in all the only thing that happens here is the planning and execution of war. How could I have missed this all these years? You see people smiling on occasion, joking with others but as I reflect on these times there's a hollowness that comes with the laughter. There's a blankness behind the smiles. I can see where meditation has been helping me to "see".

Writing a novel based on my personal Shawshank experience while working in this place will surely make for a great piece of work. I thought I could tell my story and never step foot back in this place but I will be sure to use my time here to add more substance to my writing. It's going to be okay.

3
The Old Crew

"Ava, Welcome back!"

I shouldn't be surprised that the first person I see is Maj Gen Deeds.

"Thanks Sir."

"So, was it everything I said it would be? Time away from the Beltway was exactly what you needed, right?"

"It was Sir. I just wish I could have stayed."

"Stayed? Out there? With those quacks? Oh, now Ava you wouldn't want that."

"Why wouldn't I and why would you call them quacks?"

"Because those LA types are into some really strange stuff and they're a bunch of stuck-up snobs. Surely you noticed that. You just needed the time away to recharge."

"No actually I didn't notice. I think they, unlike us here, are just into their own thing and are not concerned about what everyone else is doing. As for quacks I've learned quite a few quack'ish things that just might help me to manage being back here."

"Oh really?"

"Yes. I meditate now."

"Oh, Ava I didn't think one year would ruin you. So now you don't believe in God, huh?"

"Huh? Sir, to meditate is not to abandon your beliefs."

"Sure, that's how they get you in then the next thing you know you're in a cult. I am so glad you're back before you had time to absorb more of their quackery.

I am staring at Maj Gen Deeds in disbelief. Before I can respond he says, "Don't forget you have a Top Secret clearance. You don't want to jeopardize your career over some woo woo junk.

"Right. Well, I just need to out-process so I can start my new job on Monday."

"Where do we have you now?"

"In the same office I started in nine years ago."

"Nice!"

"What's so nice about it?"

"That means they know you've been out here learning all kinds of stuff since you left them. They want you back so they can pick that enormous brain of yours. You know, many civilians don't move around like you so there's never any new ideas in an organization. Our Air Force bubbas are trained for their specific skillsets so say a logi (logistician) will always be a logi. They will really only know what they know. You know?"

Surprisingly, Maj Gen Deeds makes sense. I hadn't thought about it from that perspective.

"Thanks Sir. That does help me see things from their point of view."

"It's what I'm here for. We'll miss you but we know how to find you!"

"Indeed, you do Sir."

Maj Gen Deeds swipes his badge and opens the door for me. We part ways with a mutual smile.

I walk into the office and see that things appear to be the same. Al rounds the corner.

"Ava!"

"Hey Al! What's up?"

"Not much. Same old thing brand new day. How was LA? Man, the year flew by quickly. Seems like just yesterday you popped in for a quick hello during your TDY."

"Yeah, I know."

"You're here to out-process, right? Col Baker said you'd be stopping by. He left a checklist for you to sign on his desk. He checked everything off himself and just needs you to sign it. He said it's not much to it since you will still be in the building just in another office."

"He's right. Just the transfer of my government travel card and update my info in the travel system to the new office which they will do."

Al and I walk into Col Baker's office. I pick up the checklist and a pen on his desk. I write a note that says I will keep my travel card and request my new office to transfer it under them. I sign the checklist and walk to the copier. As I make a copy I take one last look around.

"Aww you're going to miss us."

"Of course, I will. This directorate is crazy as shit but I got to do a lot of cool things. I am returning to the basics of aircraft maintenance. No glory in that but there is also no Marcy!"

"Ah yes! She has been on fire lately. That committee is going stale and she's taking the heat for it. Nothing is getting done but no one will dare shut it down. My guess is they will keep it on life support until they find a clever name for a new committee that does the same thing with fresh new narcissistic, power hungry, wanna be in charge of something newbie."

"I'll say a prayer for Marcy."

"A what?"

I laugh as I see the look on Al's face.

"I've been meditating this past year. It's helped me to see things differently and have a little compassion for the Marcy's of the world."

"A little compassion?"

"A little. Hey I'm still new at it so give me some time to care more deeply but yeah I see her in a different light. She's been in OSD her entire career. She has no clue of what actually goes on with any of the services and I would guess someone told her a long time ago that she didn't really need to concern herself with the details. All she needed to do was run the meetings. So, she pushes her OSD authority on others and hopes to heck we will come through with the answers she seeks to satisfy her leadership. It's really sad when you think about it."

"Well yeah, I guess so."

"Now don't get me wrong. She knows this and could do better. Could bother to learn more. Could tone down her stank attitude but she's just hiding behind some deep insecurities."

"Dang Ava."

Al reaches out his hand and places it on my forehead. I roll my eyes at him.

"I'm not sick. I am just more enlightened."

"Okay, okay. Well, I hope I can glean from your enlightened ways cause this last year has been rough and I know my attitude has plummeted even more. I'm holding you to coffee once a week so I can catch this enlightened fever you've got!"

"Sure thing!"

I grab my copy of the checklist and the original and walk back into Col Baker's office. I drop off the original and wave good-bye to Al.

So today was okay. Good insight from Maj Gen Deeds. Probably, no, most definitely the first time ever and I did feel empathy for Marcy. Hum, this is going to be okay.

I am walking through the concourse debating on buying a coffee when I see Terry.

"Ava girl!"

"Hey Terry!"

"I know you didn't just roll back into town and not tell any of us? But then again, I guess you did since we barely heard from your ass all year."

"You know I was needing to take a serious break from everything."

"Asshole Dan, yes. But your girls? Come on Ava. It's cool though. We talked about you like a dog a few times then got fussed at by Marva who told us you were on God's time and not ours. She said you were out there laying everything down at the altar.

"She was right. I needed to let it all go and you know what? I am a new me."

"Um hum and Sheryl said you seemed good when you came back for a hot minute." I see you cut off all your hair. But I did catch that in one of your Facebook posts. Is that it?"

"No, the hair is just part of it. I meditate now. I do yoga. I've had some Reiki sessions."

"Re… what? Oh, okay so you Buddha now?"

"I am at peace and I am Dan free."

"Oh, hell yeah! Okay then! I can get with that shit right there! Let's round up the girls to welcome you back and celebrate."

"Maybe next week? I just got back and I'm pretty beat from the five days of driving."

"Of course, but next week for sure."

"Yep. Well, I better get going."

"Me too. If I run, I'll get to my meeting just in time for everyone to be leaving."

"So why run?"

"Makes it look like I was hustling to get there. Like I give a shit. Don't act like you forgot that trick. You were only paroled for a year."

"Right!"

We give each other a wink and Terry begins her run walk down the hall.

I turn in the opposite direction and take a look around. There are people everywhere. Some are heading to meetings, others to the gym, some are walking around the building as their form of exercise. Still none look happy to be here. I am thankful I meditate now because without it I am sure I'd be having a nervous breakdown. It is a sweeping sense of calm that I never felt before I started my daily practice. I think though I may need to meditate more than twice a day now that I am back.

Today was a practice day but Groundhog Day begins Monday when I in-process into my new/old directorate where I started my Shawshank sentence.

Facebook, June 26, 2016

Pancake Haven. The one place where all Americans go! The old, the young the upper-class and the not, the ghetto and the redneck and everyone in between. The parking lot is an array of 20 year old Hondas and brand new BMWs. No doubt people make some effort to tolerate those not like them but on the surface, it looks like one big happy America! I am not a big fan of Pancake Haven - it's always crowded and loud and as I've matured so has my taste in cuisine. But without fail I find myself here at least twice a year usually with the excuse of its close and eggs are eggs but maybe it's because of this little spark of happiness I feel as I sit here eating my omelet and drinking my coffee. As I exit, I see an array of colors sitting on the benches waiting to be seated - squeezed in next to each other happy, talking and laughing. If only this could be us every day outside of Pancake Haven.

My observations today while at the Pancake Haven as I reflected on the presidential campaigns. I can't believe I decided to eat here the day before my return to Shawshank. I could liken it to one's last meal before execution however I hope I'd asked for something more than something off the Pancake Haven menu.

4
360 Degrees

My alarm is going off. It's 6 AM and I am hitting snooze. Please God let me keep up my meditation practice and let it be the support I need to go back in that place. The alarm goes off again and I say my prayer, "Thank you Lord for another day of living, your grace, love, mercy and support."

I take the girls for a walk and give them breakfast then make my way to the bedroom. I created a tiny meditation spot here at the foot of my bed. I have my pictures of Lord Krishna and Radha, and Lord Ganesha on the wall. On the floor are the dried flowers from my Vedic Meditation ceremony and a few candles. The small space reminds me of my meditation spot in Santa Monica only there is no partial ocean view for me to enjoy when I open my eyes.

I sit on the floor and begin to meditate. As I do I feel cool stillness sweep over me. My mouth begins to feel numb and I drift deeper into my mantra and out of body. I am lifted, light and airy. I am calm, relaxed and at peace. I wish I could stay in this space longer however my start time at Shawshank is not as flexible as it was with Big Brains Inc. so I end my meditation at thirty minutes with a few rounds of belly breathing and get up to get dressed. I smile as I pick out an outfit. Gone are the SoCal casual dress days. I am back to suits and heels but that's okay because today is a good day.

Walking to work in my bright red short sleeve skirt suit feels good too as I stay open to my *Twilight Zone* reset experience. I wish I could go back to that first year here and redo all of it. I would take the writing classes I was interested in… wait no, no, no Ava. No regrets. Everything you did got you to Santa Monica for a year and this past year has broken you open so no ma'am. No redo's but a reset is different at least to me. Perhaps the dictionary would say redo and reset are synonyms but for me reset is about seeing things from a new awareness and understanding how to move from this point of view. I have to reset my thinking about this place and see it like an object to be dissected. Much like a science class. Like the year we dissected frogs in the seventh grade. We learned about every part of those frogs, from the skin to the muscles to the organs and how they all functioned together to create life. This place is the same way – many parts functioning to create strategies, execute wars, further fueling the bureaucratic machine that drives all of us who work here crazy.

I am now standing at the door to my office knocking loudly as no one answered when I rang the buzzer. The door opens and a redhead freckled face Lieutenant Colonel is staring down at me.

"You must be Ava!"

"Hello."

"I'm Lieutenant Colonel Owens."

"Nice to meet you."

"The boss is out right now so I'll be showing you around but for starters I'll walk you over to our in-processing office so you can get that knocked out."

He opens the door and we walk ten feet to the right and land at the administrative office. He swipes in and holds the door for me. As I enter, I see five folks working at their desks. No one turns around to say hello.

"Attention!" (So completely unnecessary.)

The crew of enlisted folks quickly jump out of their seats. I can see I am going to have an interesting day with Lt Col Owens. I've already picked up on the fact that he has not offered his first name meaning he actually believes he outranks me though I am sure he knows I am a GS-14 and I am equivalent to him as far as rank is concerned. Welcome back Ava. Back to the land of egotism masking insecurities.

"Good **morning, Sir!**"

A Tech Sergeant walks up to us smiling.

"I can see you all are busy which is good but too busy to not notice who is coming through the door? Could have been Lt Gen Frank."

"You are correct Sir. Won't happen again."

"Oh no worries!"

Can someone please explain the unnecessary psychological head fucking up to me? I mean seriously you give a fuck so just stick with that. It's not about Lt Gen **Frank,** it's about you and your need to feel important. Sure, I get rank and proper acknowledgement of higher ranking officers but… but nothing Ava. You are rounding up to your first hour back in this building today and you are already smoking hot. What happened to your Zen from your meditation that was only two hours ago? Breathe.

I feel myself doing deep belly breathing as I try to focus on TSgt Carter's instructions for me filling out some paperwork. I am just noticing Lt Col Insecure is no longer with us. I wonder how long I will have to meditate before I become free of my sarcastic thoughts about this place? I feel rather calm again but damn my thoughts about these people sure haven't changed. Well, I did have some love for Marcy last week but that might have been because she wasn't physically in my presence. Maybe by my one-year meditation anniversary in December I will have achieved a deeper level of empathy for these people.

I've wrapped up my in-processing and I'm banging on the office door again. Again, Lt Col Insecure opens it.

"That was quick! I hope those guys didn't forget anything."

"I'm sure it has to do with the fact that I just out-processed from my previous office downstairs."

"Oh yeah right. You're not new to the building. I read your resume this morning, guess I forgot. That means you know your way around the place. Cool."

"Um hum."

"Okay, yeah so let me show you to your desk."

We walk through a maze of cubicles with everyone staring at me. I smile and wave though Lt Col Insecure doesn't seem to notice. Seems odd to me. Most folks introduce you as you pass through but he's just zipping on by. We make it to the far end of the office and there it is – my desk. Oh, how I am missing my office at Big Brains right now. My office with the ergonomically correct desk, chair and stool to raise my short legs up to support my posture. Here I have a mass produced ergonomic-like chair that has a gangster lean vibe going on and for lack of a better way to describe it a long ass table with a human working on the other end.

"Hello, I'm Ted your pod mate!"

"Hi Ted. I'm Ava. Nice to meet you!"

"I got everything all set up for you."

I glance back to my side of the table and notice a stack of three-inch binders labeled "Flying Hour Program". I know I will be managing this for the Air Force and there should be some part of me that is excited to manage a major part of the Air Force's operations but I really don't care. I don't care about the cost of fuel, flightline maintenance for our fleets or anything else that falls under this program. I am here to study and observe and get my novel completed.

"Thanks Ted."

Ted begins to say something but Lt Col Insecure interrupts him.

"Since you're not new to the building I will spare you the grand tour."

I am quite sure I have a no shit look on my face as I glance at Lt Col Insecure. I take a moment to read his badge and notice his first name is Michael.

"No need for that Michael or do you go by Mike? You're a logi so I'm guessing you don't have a call sign, right?"

He is speechless. He composes himself and finally says, "Mike."

I smile satisfied with his answer and turn back to Ted. Mike walks away.

"How long have you worked here?"

"I've been in this office for five years. I'm a retired Lt Col who was lucky to get on as a contractor, see."

Ted is pointing out the slight difference in his badge that brands him as a contractor. As I look more closely at his badge, I can see he's lost quite a bit of hair since the picture was taken. Our badges expire on a regular basis so I know the picture is not that old. Ted has gone from a head full of jet-black hair to a receding hairline. I see too that his complexion is different. Perhaps he had a tan in the badge photo because he's now as pale as snow. I hope he is okay and doesn't have any health issues.

I catch myself deep in thought as I notice Ted staring at me staring at him. I try to play it off as if I am pondering his last words.

"That's great you were able to get on as a contractor."

"I guess though a part of me thinks I should have looked for something else. My wife thinks so. She says not taking a break from this place is what aged me so badly."

Ted laughs and I just received confirmation about how deadly this place is for the soul.

Facebook, June 27, 2016

I did it!!! I survived my first day back in the Pentagon! But...I did have California on my mind all day ✳☺✳. Can't wait to return to CA on a full-time basis but happy to be here now cause God's plans have always proven to be better than mine ☺ I'm looking forward to what's to come here in the great DMV!

Such a positive post though as I left work this evening I wondered if this is how repeat offenders feel when they return to jail. Only for me I don't feel like I did anything wrong. I've been sent back here because someone didn't care, didn't give a fuck about me or my career or the fact that I signed a mobility agreement for goodness sakes and could be anywhere else in the world. I am recalling Maj Gen Deed's thought's about why I am back to square one and it helps but it also doesn't.

I know meditation is supposed to be helping me feel better and be in a positive mood and finding my internal joy but damn if this place doesn't suck the life out of me. I've been in here twice since my return and today was hard. The funky ass attitudes of superiority. The racist bullshit that has been here since its inception. Heck that's why there are so many restrooms in this place because it was built during the days of segregation and truthfully, we still are segregated by race, rank, class (military, civilian, contractor), favoritism, nepotism, sexism. Nope, not one damn thing has changed in the many decades since.

I've got to triple down on my meditation if this is going to work. I recall Nala saying meditation doesn't remove your sense of shitty people or your desire to curse on occasion. I guess if anything I have a better sense of people because I meditate. I can definitely feel my intuition getting stronger so I am sure my vibes about people are part of this heightened awareness.

Facebook, June 29, 2016

Going through a bunch of things I hadn't looked through in years and came across this. Do you guys remember?

During my minimizing as part of my great return to California, I ran across a few photos of my college friends and me from our freshman year. Looking back, I'd never believe everything that's happened to me has occurred. From being date raped a few months after these photos were taken to dating the crack addict boyfriend in Oklahoma to emails with the creator of one of the most popular television shows of the 90s while I was out in California. I do know I am here in this lifetime to do something spectacular. I say this not with any vanity but with assurance. No one goes through shit to end up with just a basic shitty life. Well, I guess one can but for those who are determined to understand their purpose for being here I can't see us settling for just being happy we are alive. I want and I deserve more than that. Everyone does.

Facebook, July 1, 2016

The bureaucracy is real and painful if you let it get to you but... meditation. The reason I made it through the entire week! Thank you Nala my God sent meditation teacher!!!

I am feeling much better. I've tripled up on my meditations one before work one right after work and one a little bit later in the evening. It's bringing me back to my sense of calm and peace that I felt when I was out in California. This is going to be needed to deal with these people. These people have no clue how lost they are. They have no clue as to how enslaved they have made themselves. Or maybe they do and they just want to pretend like this isn't affecting them. I'm not sure just yet but I will be doing my investigative reporting. This book will free me and I need to be freed.

5
Happy Hour

I'm sticking to my promise to meet the girls for happy hour. I've run into all of them during my first week back. Jamie and I carved out time for lunch together but this will be a long overdue and much needed evening with all the girls.

I spent so much time alone last year that it feels a bit overwhelming just thinking about meeting up. I rather enjoyed my solitude and I have a feeling this is going to be how I am moving forward. Not that I don't enjoy my girls but they can be a lot and I know none of them are down with anything I learned over the last year and Sheryl made that very clear when I was back in town a few months ago.

But here I am and heck I just survived my first week back at Shawshank so I deserve this Happy Hour. I wonder though if I will ever stop calling it Shawshank? Doubtful.

I stop just shy of the entrance and step back a few feet. I find the acupressure point that is supposed to help me with anxiety on my left wrist and hold for a few minutes as I inhale and exhale slowly. Tammy taught me this and it works like a charm. I'm not particularly anxious just expecting the usual from the crew. There will be questions about Dan, what the hell I was doing all year, why I ghosted them even though Terry said Mavra told them why. And I know Sheryl has given her two cents to the group.

I close my eyes tightly then open them and walk up to the entrance. I barely have the door cracked open and I can tell I am going to want to jet in less than an hour. The music is loud, people are tightly packed around the bar and while Terry texted and said she snagged a table upstairs the good of not getting constantly bumped into at the bar is not outweighing the comfortable seating at a table mainly because they will want to stay longer. I will have to remind myself that that's what they want and what they do has nothing to do with me and how long I want to be here tonight.

I begin my ascent up the staircase and as I reach the top I see Terry, Dana, Jamie and Sheryl. I am a bit surprised I am the last one here.

"Hey Ava, long time no see," says Dana. Jamie gives me a big grin.

"Hey!"

They stand as I make my way to them and we have a quick group hug. Sheryl stays seated waiting for me to acknowledge her.

"Hi Sheryl."

"Hello. I feel like the privileged one since I'm the only one who's seen you over the last 12 months."

"Yes, that was a lovely night when I was back here for a quick trip for Big Brains."

"Terry, thanks as always for bringing us together."

I walk over to Terry wrap my arms around her shoulders as she too remains seated.

"You're welcome. You know we were not going to let you just slide back in the DMV and not have a reunion."

"I know and thanks for giving me time to get settled in. No Marva?"

Terry chuckles.

"Is there ever a Marva at Happy Hour?"

"No. I guess it has been some years since she's joined us."

"Girl if it ain't for Jesus, Marva ain't joining us," Dana laughs.

"I should be like Marva, says Sheryl."

"You are damn near close," says Dana.

"I think you can be for Jesus and gin." Jamie holds up her glass and she and Dana click their glasses together.

I take my seat at the round table and Terry hands me the Happy Hour menu.

"Okay," says Dana. "Let's get into it? How many celebrities did you see? Did you go shopping on Rodeo Drive? I know you went to Beverly Hills!"

I look up from the menu and smile. The waiter is now standing next to me and I order a glass of Chardonnay and the fully loaded nachos. I then begin to speak but Sheryl interrupts me.

"Dana really. Ava was out there on a prestigious fellowship. She was not out there taking Hollywood tours and hanging out on Rodeo Drive."

"Actually, I did go on a Hollywood tour of homes and of course I drove through Beverly Hills a few times and I didn't do any shopping on Rodeo Drive but I did drive down it."

"Sheryl rolls her eyes."

"I thought you were out there furthering your career. And I do hope you severed ties from whoever those cult people were that were putting those crazy ideas in your head."

Terry peers over at Sheryl with a quizzical look.

"Say what now?"

"I wasn't part of a cult. Sheryl is referring to my *Eat Pray Love* experience."

"Aww that sounds nice," says Jamie. "Did you have a spiritual awakening?"

"Jamie, please!"

"What Sheryl? Many people have them. I think we're all supposed to have one at some point."

I smile as I press hard on the acupressure point on my wrist.

Terry can see I am already drained from Sheryl.

"Hey Sheryl, tell you what, why don't we let Ava get in a few sips of her wine before we condemn her to hell."

My attention was so focused on my acupressure point I hadn't noticed the waiter had brought my glass of Chardonnay. I pick it up and smile at Terry. I raise my glass to simulate cheers. I take a sip and then another. As I place the glass on the table I look Sheryl square in the face.

"I don't expect you or anyone for that matter to understand my journey but I do expect you to respect me."

"Okay, well that's fair," says Dana.

"Agree," says Terry.

Sheryl is pissed. She is used to saying whatever she likes with no consequences. She holds herself on this pedestal that we all know is fake as shit but we never challenge her about it. Today I have decided not to challenge her misgivings but to use my Throat Chakra and stand up for myself. I feel powerful and I know my Solar Plexus Chakra is on fire as well.

Jamie breaks the silence.

"Ava, I am happy for you. You deserve to have the best experiences in life."

"Thank you, Jamie."

"Amen to that," says Dana.

I pick up the menu and try to focus on the selections and to block Sheryl's disapproving glare.

"How are we doing ladies?"

I look up at the waiter and smile.

"We are doing great. You know, I think I'll also have the cheesecake."

"Sure thing ma'am."

"I thought you spiritual types were vegan. I guess you're still learning the ropes."

"That is a misconception. Look Sheryl, I know when we met up the other month you were concerned about some of the new experiences I was having and I get that but I am going to say this one more time. Let it go. This is my life, not yours. The way I connect with God and my Spirit Team is not your concern."

"Fine. I won't say another word."

"Good, says Dana. You've said enough already. Now back to the fun stuff! Girl, please tell me you ran into Shemar Moore!"

"Nope but I did see a few celebrities and I was on two television shows."

"Now that's what I'm talking about!"

Dana, Terry and Jamie lean in to hear my tales of Hollywood as Sheryl pulls her phone out of her purse and leaves the table.

I'm sure she will return with an excuse as to why she has to leave but I am not going to concern myself with her antics this evening. I know my time in California was healing and I got to a place I never reached in traditional therapy. God has many ways to support us and mine comes by way of what the world refers to as alternative healing. Though I am not sure it should be called alternative since everything is something that was here long before manufactured drugs and schools issuing out degrees in psychology. Seems like the modern way to heal would be called alternative but then that would be logical and when has logic ever made its way into the way this world operates?

Facebook, July 10, 2016

Today marks 21 years of federal service! All with the Air Force and starting my ninth year at the Headquarters.

The Pentagon. The mystery building for many has been a place that has served me well and unlocked truths in me as I served to support our country's mission as a civilian.

It's been here that ironically, I opened my heart to accept my gift of writing and transitioning that gift into a full-time career and it was because of the fantastic fellowship this past year that I really started pursuing my dream and connecting with those in the field. It is also where I met some amazing, wonderful positive thinking people who inspired me and helped me grow spiritually!

Yes, the two are as opposite as night and day; our nation's defense and a professional writing career but God has awesome ways of linking things up!

I could've never guessed when I graduated from Alabama State University in the spring of 1995 all the wonderful things that would occur throughout these 21 years.

I remember being told in college by my professors that I should change my major to English but I was headset on having what I considered to be a "professional career" so accounting it was. But all things work out for the best and all my life experiences certainly find their way into my writing. And what's more interesting is I've been writing since I was seven and haven't stopped. Now it's time to take it to the next level!!!

I am thankful for my ASU crew, my Tinker crew, my Pentagon crew, my CA crew and all my family and friends who support me, encourages me and on occasion party heavily with me 😁

I know I'm still at the beginning of this journey and there is more to discover while here on this earth in this body and I'm looking forward to every single day!!!!

Happy Sunday!!!!

This is such a fucked up post. I should have told the truth which is I fucking hate working at the Pentagon and I am sad that I've been self-enslaved for 21 years. Thankful though for the money and the stability which again is part of that enslavement we've all bought into but for the most part I don't want to be here not even to finish the novel.

There's pain here. The pain of where Dan and I met. The pain of the Groundhog bureaucratic bullshit. It's the pain of knowing that I have never once not in one day of this entire 21 fucking years wanted to do any of it. How miserable is it to know you've spent your entire adult life doing something you can't stand?

I am certain I am not the only one. There are others with jobs they hate, spouses they can't stand, churches they wish they didn't attend… the list goes on.

Anyway, it's Sunday and that means a nice drive out to Mount Vernon trail with Cleo and Sophie. We will sit by the bank of the Potomac River, get our Earthing in and reset before the hell of Shawshank begins tomorrow.

6
Practicing Better OPSEC (Operational Security)

It's a beautiful warm morning and I am heading back to my apartment with Cleo and Sophie. As I wait for the light to change a car pulls up. The window rolls down and I see a black man smiling at me.

"Hello pretty lady."

Way too early in the morning for this.

"Hello"

I smile and look ahead hoping the light will change.

"You know I've seen you **every day on my way to work and I** thought today is the day I am going to say hello."

"Oh?"

"Yes, so I was wondering if I could get your number, maybe take you out some time."

"I don't think…"

"**Oh yeah,** I know this is kind of creepy but look here's my **government badge. I work here** in Crystal City. I promise you I'm not a stalker."

He's holding his badge up like he's FBI or something.

"Well, you kind of disproved that when you told me you've been seeing me for days."

"I can see your point but hey how about if I give you my number and you call me if you're comfortable."

The fact that I am standing here having this conversation with this man on a fairly empty street at 6:30 AM must tell me I am either way too trusting or perhaps he's okay.

I see him writing his number down. He leans over the passenger seat and hands me his business card.

I flip it over to find his cell phone number on the back.

"See that's where I work so you should feel more comfortable now."

I wonder if he is unaware of the many violent attacks that have occurred over the years by men who were in the military. Fort Hood to name one. How does being a government employee make you harmless? Just the same I am still standing here so there's that.

I smile.

"We'll see. Have a nice day."

"You too pretty lady."

I've got to practice better OPSEC. Seriously he's seen me for days and I never noticed the same car coming down this street every day, especially when there are only a hand full of cars on 15th street at this hour of the day.

Anyway, I doubt if I call him. He's not very attractive and honestly, I have not thought about dating. I have come to accept that whatever that was with Dan was whack as shit and I was desperately trying to make it something to avoid having to meet anyone. I am not of fan of the dating process so I just settled into quite possibly the most dysfunctional thing I could conjure up and then hoped and prayed it would last until death do us part. I will say between meditating, Reiki, hypnosis and rediscovering my common sense which I am sure is directly tied to daily meditation I am over Dan.

Facebook, August 20, 2016

Going through some old photos and feeling good. This little girl had no clue where life would take her but so far, she's had some pretty cool adventures. I now know she was born to fulfill a purpose and is blessed with the gifts to get it done!!! And I need to take a lesson from her because she knew how to relax!

Seeing this picture of me at a year and a half wearing a yellow dress and black patent leather shoes with my legs crossed looking down chilling on a lounge chair in front of my grandparents' house you would think that this little girl had a dream childhood. So again another Facebook post lie because the truth of the matter is I was born into a loveless marriage with an older sister who would always be the favorite. But I think maybe, just maybe this little girl had already figured this out or rather she still remembered what her purpose was. It's like what Marva says we all make a soul contract with God before we arrive on this earth. It's the thought that we know what this is for some time and then as we get older, we forget. Life, parents, family in general clog our little brains and we forget our purpose.

Yeah, looking deeply at this photo, this little girl is self-assured and wise. She is thinking about the battles in the war she will fight and she knows she is likely to soon forget her purpose but she also knows when the time is right, she will remember and she will WIN!

I am recalling my hypnosis session with Amy. I allow myself time to reflect on my life. The memories are haunting yet there is peace in me. I healed a great deal from that session. Going back and comforting my younger Avas was needed and I still remember that I am big Ava protecting all the little Avas. I know that part of protecting means accomplishing the great escape from Shawshank.

Okay Sally Hemings. You've showed up twice and both times I've asked what I am to learn from you. I know you will show me soon and I have to think it has something to do with how to free myself from this career. Perhaps there's more than just the writing of my novel for me to do? I am open and I am ready to receive from you.

7
The Date

His name is Mason and we're meeting at **Casual Days an Americana** restaurant. I am already turned off by this and yes, it's because I am boujee. I am 43 years old and this is where my date is taking me? Surely, I have more to look forward to in my mid-forties than this. This could quite possibly be worse than steak and sex at Dan's condo.

I enter the restaurant dressed in a simple knee-high black dress and strappy black shoes. To my surprise there is a DJ and a whole club scene happening. I didn't know this was a thing. Mason, my date stands and greets me.

He yells, "Ms. Pretty Lady. Happy Friday to you!"

I smile as I take him in. He is at least six feet tall, very slender with the roundest head I've ever seen. His complexion is about that of milk chocolate and his nose and lips are rather broad though if they were any smaller, they would look odd on his round face.

Why am I doing this again? To get out? To meet some nice men? I certainly can't meet them in my apartment.

The hostess walks us to our table and hands us menus. The music is so loud I feel as though I could crawl out of my skin. I can't do this. Mason notices my discomfort.

"Hey, I see this is not your thing. What would you like to do instead?"

"Someplace much quieter would be great."

"Sure. I know a spot just down the road. You can follow me there."

"Okay."

"We stand to leave just as the waitress approaches our table."

"You guys heading out already?"

"Yeah I'm 0 for 1 for our first date."

"Aww. So sorry but hey we only have music on the weekends so be sure to come back another time!"

I give her a pleasant smile and follow Mason out the door. And by follow, I mean follow. Dude didn't hold the door open for me. Two strikes and I should get in my car and drive home but I have to get back out here, I guess.

We are in the parking lot and he finally stops.

"This is my ride."

I wonder if he recalls how we met? Maybe he has me confused with someone else.

I look at his Audi then look up at him.

"Yes, it's nice. I recall thinking that when we first met."

"Ah yeah right!"

I follow Mason up the street and to my surprise we are in a strip mall parking lot. I am familiar with it as I shop here all the time and was not aware of any restaurants but I park next to his car and get out. As I do I see a line of people waiting to go inside one of the stores.

A club? I have seen this place and never thought about what it was though in retrospect I have seen the sign that simply says café but never gave it any thought. Mason motions for me to join him and we walk side by side and join the line of people. I can hear the music blasting from here so I am not sure how this is different than disco night at Casual Days.

"I think this is exactly your speed!"

"Really?"

"Yeah, don't let the music fool you. Once you're inside you'll see what I mean."

I am believing I won't see what he means but I got dressed and came out tonight so I will go along with this for a bit longer.

We are now at the entrance and I see the person taking the cover charge has a gun. I am both intrigued and fearful. The money taker/bouncer looks at us and Mason looks at me. I know he does not think I am paying to get in here. I turn my head and stare into the club. Mason pulls out his wallet and pays.

We enter into hell.

The place is like nothing I've ever seen before. Tables full of people smoking hookahs and others dancing to Puff Daddy's music and yes, I mean when Diddy was Daddy. I am all for some throwback music and I know Diddy is on tour with his Bad Boy Reunion but… nope. I don't think they are paying homage to Diddy, Mase and the reunion tour.

We find our way to an empty table and I have gone from what the fuck to amused. A waitress comes over and asks for our drink orders.

I order a whisky sour. Might as well since I've entered a time warp. Mason orders a vodka neat. I'm guessing he expects me to pay for these drinks since he handled the cover charge.

He yells, "Better, right?"

"No," I yell back.

He honestly looks confused.

"Why? We've got nice music and…"

He stops midsentence to order a hookah from a waitress walking by.

"Do you smoke?"

"No, I don't. Thank you though."

"Yeah so, we've got nice music, nice ambiance. You said you meditate so this is your kind of vibe, right?"

I should stop telling people I meditate because clearly many have exceptionally odd understandings about the practice.

"Honestly, this is just like Casual Days with no food."

"How can you say that?"

"Because we're at a club."

"Yes, with hookahs. Nice chill vibe. I told you I got you!"

Dear God. OPSEC Ava, OPSEC! You could have avoided this entire nightmare.

The waitress brings our drinks and the hookah he ordered. I watch him light it and begin puffing.

"Do you do this often?"

"Yeah, but not here as often as I used to because now, I have one of these at home."

"Sure."

I smile and down my drink in a few seconds. Mason seems impressed. I stand and lean over to yell in his ear.

"Thank you for trying, however I don't feel as though we are on the same page regarding what a date looks like."

"Wow, so you're leaving."

"Yes, I am."

He stands and leans over to give me a hug. I think about leaving a few bucks for my drink and decide against it. I turn to leave and as I do I say a silent prayer.

Dear God, please get me out of here and into my car safely. Thank you.

I make it to my car and before I drive off, I can't help but laugh.

"Well, you're back out here in these dating streets and you are going to give yourself major credit for tonight!"

I drive out of the parking lot to head home. Next time will be better. Positive thoughts!

Facebook, Sep 18, 2016

At Freakazoid. Round 2!!! I love this exercise class! Sunday is two classes for the price of 1 so 2 hours of awesomeness 😄 *Committed to being fit and fabulous in my 40s!!!*

Since I'm back in these dating streets I am not only wanting to look good for me but hey I know some men like a nice body and honestly, I think they deserve to have that from their woman as she may want that from her man.

I have myself to look sexy for at the moment and that is just fine with me. Mr. Just Like Stedman will come soon enough. I have gotten a few looks and been asked for my number but right now I am in introspection mode. After the hookah hood'ness a couple weeks ago I'm back in these dating streets but I am proceeding with caution!

I have to admit the writing and clearing out my things is going slower than I'd imagined. I feel like there's a vortex that is slowly sucking me back into the Shawshank cray-cray. I must fight it though. I can't conform to complacency. It's unfair to me and to all those I am supposed to support through my writing. I know this but still the proverbial quicksand is real and it produces a massive quantity of inertia.

Meditating does help and I am feeling more connected to my purpose to educate inspire and entertain through my gift as a writer but man still struggling to push through. How can I know what lies ahead and not go charging forth to get it? It's like being attracted to people who are just as dysfunctional as your family or something like that. There is a weird ass comfort with the Pentagon. My life is really like "The Shawshank Redemption". Can't be Red. Must be Andy.

I should reach out to Amy for a Reiki session.

Facebook, September 20, 2016

Just strolled back from a training session at the Office of Personnel Management and had the pleasure of zigzagging through the streets that make up George Washington University. It was so nice to see the young, happy faces of the students. Do I miss my college days? Heck no!!! But seeing them talking, laughing, enjoying life pre full-time employment did bring a smile to my face. As I neared the metro, I saw them. The suited up serious-minded Washingtonians - what they look like... life post GW -my how they vary from those laid back SoCal folks I was with for the last year. Then I laughed as I realized I have morphed back (look-wise) into this. I'm in my black suit, hair is on point and...heels! Thank God I will always be in harmony with my California state of mind ☺ Meditation -can't make it without it! Wonder how much people would react if I came in tomorrow in my Converse, jeans and t-shirt??? But I'm blessed with employment so it's best to rock the D.C. federal employee style.

I am not sure what this post is actually saying except perhaps I need both Amy and Dr. Smith. Not because I need to figure out what I want out of life as I now know this but why in the hell do I use Facebook as some kind of therapy blog?

I do know that I don't want to be an SES (Senior Executive Service Member) and coming to this training today solidified that for me. It helped me to see how much my leadership has used me over the years. The instructor made it clear that if your leadership is comfortable allowing you to meet with top leadership, take their meetings and other SESs and/or general officers feel comfortable with you running these meetings and have no problem picking up the phone to discuss an issue with you well then, you've been played. She said sure it feels good that they are letting you run the show but the fact of the matter is if you are doing all of this you SHOULD be an SES. You SHOULD be the one getting the big salary and the recognition. I guess what she said didn't surprise me but it certainly helped me to put my 21-year career into perspective.

Maybe I should come to work in Chuck Taylors and jeans tomorrow. I wonder why I give a fuck? This really isn't me and what I learned while in California amongst many things is that even these clothes are restrictive. Sure, I look cute as hell when I bebop around in my tiny little suits my cute four inch heels and don't get me wrong I love a cute shoe but the rest of this garb is just not me. I did the big chop with my hair in California but now I'm back to wearing weave or rather the newest thing, crochet braids trying to fit in trying to blend in again not because I necessarily feel self-conscious about the big chop and the natural hair but it's almost like I need to put this disguise back on so that maybe it'll numb the pain of being here.

I am slowly starting to lose the zeal to clear things out and get ready to move back. I haven't heard from any of the companies I applied to back in California - not an interview, not a rejection, nothing. But I have to remember I wasn't ready to stay out there so there must be some reason I'm back, something that was tugging at my heart to return to this place. I do hope I discover it soon because being here is slowly breaking me down again.

I just picked up my package from the concierge desk. I ordered Stephen King's *Different Seasons* which is a collection of four of his novellas as I want to see how he crafts these stories. I am mostly interested in reading *Rita Hayworth and Shawshank Redemption* as I've nicknamed the Pentagon Shawshank and I am a fan of the movie adaptation. I'm thinking of turning my novel into three novellas because I have been reading that the average reader is no longer a fan of expansive novels. I had the package shipped to me as a gift. I open it and read my note to myself.

There's no one standing in your way. Go Ava, go!

I am a good talented loveable smart and special person. This is something others see in me yet I had not been accepting of these qualities about myself. People love my writing and have always encouraged me to write more. I've had literary agents ask me to send them excerpts from my work, got encouraging feedback from another agent for Cleo and Sophie's book. It was me who was holding on to self-doubt from the way I was treated as a child. I now understand more that this is my job to heal and to move into a new light. I owe it to me and my little Avas to go! I am a work in progress and I am loving the journey.

Facebook, September 21, 2016

Post: Relax everything is running right on schedule – the Universe

I can see I needed this reminder.

Facebook, Sep 22, 2016

About to get turnt up with P Diddy and the family! Can't believe I'm at the Bad Boy Reunion concert and on a work night but I couldn't miss this!

I am with Dana and Terry. The only place in the DMV where anyone should hear old music by P Diddy. I still have flashbacks of that hookah club. I can only imagine Mason was there for hours. He called the other week and I just stared at the phone. One thing I am doing better at is recognizing bullshit and steering clear of it as opposed to my old M.O. of running towards it with open arms.

This music is taking me back! Back to when I was much younger and thought nothing about time, getting older and my soul's purpose. I have never been happy with my career as a federal employee but there was a time when I did the work and enjoyed my free time away from my job. I've always made good money so there was this understanding that this was what I had to do to enjoy the lifestyle I had. The luxury apartments and later home purchases. It wasn't until my time in California that I saw what I could have which is so much more than a nice six-figure salary. I could have my enjoyment of writing and living out my soul's purpose and heck I could be living in Malibu shopping on Rodeo Drive. The energy exchange of money for my writing can yield so much more and I would be in my purpose and in my big house.

"Ava girl, shake your ass!"

Dana is tugging on my arm and bringing me back to the present moment.

I shake my head to clear my thoughts and begin dancing to *Mo Money Mo Problems* rather ironic considering I was daydreaming of my bomb writing career and Malibu mansion.

Facebook, Sep 24, 2016

About to see Stephen King!!! And later Kareem Abdul Jabbar and Shonda Rhimes - the queen of prime-time television and now published author. I've come to the National Book Festival for years always daydreaming of the day I would be one of the authors speaking and God has blessed me to move closer to that dream becoming a reality! I'm loving experiencing my dream unfold!

I guess this post only means something to me as anyone else reading it has no freaking clue what I'm talking about since I am not really working on this book like I said I would. Sitting five feet away from Stephen King today and about 20 feet away from Shonda Rhimes and Kareem Abdul Jabbar was wonderful and inspiring however I need to be writing. I need to be doing what I need to be doing so that I can actually be on this stage so that I can share my story, my truth. I know I'm called to do this. I know this is what I'm supposed to be doing. I know this is my purpose. I want my books to turn into movies just like Stephen King and they can't do that if I don't write them.

Facebook, Sep 24, 2016

What an amazing day! God is so great! I came for a couple of reasons - Stephen King and Shonda Rhimes and was happy to see Kareem Abdul-Jabbar while I was here but he by far was the one I needed to hear from today. God always knows best! To top off my day I'm in line waiting for Holly Robinson Peete to sign my book. This week has been very eclectic. P Diddy and the Bad Boy Reunion and all the wonderful authors today. But it's not their celebrity that moves me it's their hard work and dedication that inspires me!

Does it really though because I'm not doing shit. I've gotta do shit! I've been sucked back into the vortex of Shawshank and for the love I can't move. I'm still meditating but I'm certainly not writing every day. I'm not cleaning out all this stuff that I don't need and there's a part of my desire to return to California that's fading more and more and while I know that I am here to learn something and to be the roving reporter I said I was going to be to write this book, I also know I'm supposed to be back there. For nearly 20 years God has given me a vision of a man and a Malibu beach house. I am always on the phone talking to my editor. As soon as I hang up, the love of my life calls and says he's on his way home. I've never seen his face but I know he's out there and I don't know how the hell we're going to get together if I can't get my shit together so that I can be in Malibu in my beach house. Perhaps I'm just crazy but I honestly don't think so. God has made it very clear that this is for me and yet I'm not moving forward. Something is blocking me and I've got to figure out what that is.

Facebook, September 24, 2016

And my day is DONE😁😁😁 From these pictures you'd think Holly Robinson Peete and I go way back!

So let me get this right, I woke up this morning. I came down to the Convention Center. I was five feet away from Stephen King and heard his inspirational story. I listened to Kareem Abdul Jabbar and Shonda Rhimes, heard their inspiring stories went downstairs and not only did I meet Holly Robinson Peete and she signed her book for me but we literally had a conversation!

I am fired up and yet unmotivated at all at the same time. Here these people are doing what they were called to this earth to do and here I am just sitting here watching them getting inspired but yet deep in my heart knowing that there's something I've got to clear so that I too can live out my purpose. It was just a few months ago that I was in the same city as Holly Robinson Peete and Shonda Rhimes as I'm fairly certain they both live in the LA area now here they are in D.C. to speak to us. I want to be that person. I want to be the one traveling, speaking, inspiring others. I know I need to stick with my meditation. I know that's the key. I know the answers will come though I didn't think that moving back here would be so debilitating to my soul but I can see that it has been.

Colonel Baker said I needed to get out of the Beltway for a while but I don't know anyone who should be here on a fulltime basis. The DMV is so heavy. It's not just the Pentagon, it's The Hill, the lobbyist, the news networks. The people here are living under a dark low vibrational stain that can't ever be cleansed.

Facebook, October 6, 2016

At the National Museum of African American History and Culture. Grateful for those who sacrificed, for those who inspire us today, and for those who worked to bring all of this beautiful and diverse history into this amazing space- thank you!!!

More of my purpose for returning here was revealed to me today and it happened while I was in front of the lunch counter exhibit. I have more to give to the people here. Here I am in this breathtaking museum and there's not one thing here that didn't shape me in some way. If not me directly then someone who has affected me or someone who impacted them or some degree of separation but just the same this is my history. I don't know who these people will be but I hear God telling me to hold on just a little bit longer. Give me just a little more time and I'll take you back to LA. Okay God. I will try my best to be patient and listen to you. I do wonder though what is it? Why am I back here? My faith will keep me holding on.

8
My Date with Sally Hemings

I woke up at 6 AM this morning and I am driving to Monticello which is about two hours away in Charlottesville. It's time I go and meet with one of my ancestors, Sally Hemings. She has a message for me and she has made it clear I need to hear it at TJ's (Thomas Jefferson) home. I purchased the last ticket for the Hemings tour last night, something I didn't realize was offered but I see things have changed since I was last at Monticello. I read that the Jefferson foundation has now acknowledged Sally and Jefferson's children as his. I think some see this as a victory. I see it as common sense.

I know I am not here for a deeper education on Jefferson's lineage, at least it doesn't feel like I am. I've reached the parking lot and I am just in time to pick up my ticket and board the bus that takes you to the house. I am tickled at the conversation that is taking place behind me on the bus. A white mother and her daughter who is around ten years old are discussing Thomas Jefferson not freeing his slaves when he died.

Mother: "You know Thomas Jefferson didn't free all of his slaves when he died."

Daughter: "I'm sure there was a good reason."

Mother: "Maybe they didn't want to be free."

Daughter: "That seems unlikely."

(Me, thinking): This is going to be a long day and I am the only black person on this bus.

We exit the bus and I listen for the tour guides to tell us where to go for the various tours. The Hemings tour will be under the big tree just down the way.

I know this tree. I recall sitting on the bench a few years ago after I toured Monticello. I walk over and see a handful of people waiting. We smile at each other and remain quiet. A few minutes later our tour guide arrives. She starts off with the shock and awe fact that Sally was Jefferson's sister-in-law. That Jefferson's wife and Sally were **half-sisters due to** the fact that Jefferson's father-in-law rape Sally's mother. No, the tour guide didn't say these words but it's my theory. I refuse to romanticize the raping of enslaved women. I also have a hard time believing the Jefferson - Hemings love affair. Stockholm syndrome perhaps but that's the best I can offer to why anyone would believe it was a consensual relationship.

But as usual, I digress.

I hear the tour guide pointing out the rolling hills of Monticello.

"As you can see, this place is a wonderland! Just imagine spending the day running throughout the hills enjoying this beautiful countryside!"

I chuckle. I guess I could imagine this assuming I was white in another lifetime because my black ass would not have been running anywhere. I would have been working my ass off and if it looked like I was running I can only imagine there would be a pack of white men with dogs chasing after me because surely they would think I was trying to escape.

I have all but tuned out the tour guide as I am lost in my twisted since of humor when I hear a whisper in my ear.

"But ain't you acting like that now?"

"Sally?"

"You's as free as you can get but you acting like you's me back on this plantation."

I turn slowly and there she is, again. Sally Hemings has graced me with her presence for the third time and this time I am on her turf. Twice before I have only allowed myself to see her from my peripheral vision but today, I turn and face her. I see the tour group starting to move towards the house and I walk slowly behind them with Sally by my side. I say nothing. I think nothing. I just walk.

"They gonna take you in here and show you how my people lived. They gonna tell you some great stories of how good, reliable and faithful my family was to this place. They gonna tell you how grateful Thomas Jefferson was for us. And they gonna tell you how I was by his side when he died. And I am telling you not one of us had a choice in the matter. Do you hear me?"

Sally's voice is slightly raised above the whisper she was originally speaking in. I look at her as the tour group enters the back of the house.

"Stop acting like you's me cause you ain't."

She fades away and I am left with very little to process because she gave it to me straight. I could spin out of control and think I've lost my mind. Or I could be super excited to have had such a divine connection and I am of course but mostly I am ashamed. She is right.

There is nothing holding me to my plantation but me and mine is a mental plantation created by the lack of belief in myself.

I continue on with the group. I listen intently to everything the guide explains about life as a Hemings. The jobs they did and where they did them – mostly in this dungeon looking space. After the tour I make my way down Mulberry Row, the place where Jefferson's slaves among others (free blacks, whites etc.) performed various jobs. I continue on to the cemetery where I stand looking through the gate at Jefferson's grave. I don't see her but I know Sally is right beside me. We then walk back up Mulberry Row and make our way to the site where the reconstructed slave cabin stands. I walk inside and cry. So small and housing over 10 people or more.

What the hell is wrong with you Ava? Get your shit together, write the damn novel and get free. Sounds so easy and yet I know there is a fear in me that is burning fiercely. It is here in this place that I found the understanding of why I have slowed down my return to California. It is the desire to be free coupled with the fear of the unknown. Just like Jefferson's slaves. That mother on the bus saying maybe they didn't want to be free might be correct. Maybe they were afraid of what lay ahead and if given the choice many would have opted to stay enslaved. I see now that's my issue. It's not the desire to be free it's the what in the hell do I do with my freedom and how uncomfortable it will be to actually be free.

I understand now I have more work to do. I do know that for each passing day I meditate I am more certain of my purpose but I am scared to move out on it. I will stay open God and do the work whatever it is because I know my freedom lies in being free. Thank you, Sally.

9
Reiki

I am sitting in the same room I was in a year ago. Amy smiles warmly at me.

"I can't **believe** it's been a year since my first session."

"Yes, and you are still vibrating very high."

"I am?"

"Yes, I can feel it. You were when you came back into town a few months ago and you still are."

"I am not feeling like I did then. I feel like I waited too long to come see you."

"No, you are right on time."

"Really?"

"Ava, I've mentioned this before. You are a healer. Even if you are going through something you have been blessed with this beautiful gift that supports you. So even if you are feeling a bit down, the power of God running through you is strong. You may feel lower than you did a year ago but you are light years away from the dark energy that was with you then. Does this make sense?"

"Not really. I feel the heaviness of this area and it weighs on me. I have something very important to accomplish and up until a recent visit to Monticello I was dragging my feet."

"And the trip to Monticello gave you motivation?"

"Yes, in a very unusual way. I saw the ghost of a slave and she gave me a good talking to about how I was holding myself back. That I was in my own way."

"That's so lovely! You're back on track."

I shouldn't be surprised Amy is not remotely concerned about what I just shared. I am still learning about Reiki and the power of energy healing and while she's not a medium like Mona (a least I don't think she is) I just know somehow all of this alternative stuff is connected.

"As for why you think you are vibrating low, well that has to do with the fact that you are an empath. You feel deeply the emotions of others. And, in this area you are feeling the heaviness of the Beltway. So much darkness happens here, crime, corruption, laws and policies passed that don't reflect the needs of many in this country. It's important you begin to learn to distinguish your feelings from the energy you are absorbing. While you are doing great with keeping your vibration high you can begin to experience lower vibrations if you are unable to clear this heavy energy from your energy field. It's like cleaning a mirror. If we don't, over time there is a film that doesn't allow us to clearly see and our reflection is dull. I'll show you how to do that today."

"Thanks for that explanation. It makes sense. Being out of the Beltway for a year was liberating and the energy on the West Coast is so much lighter than here. I am meditating three times a day so I guess that helps."

"It most certainly does. It's like you've super activated your spiritual gifts by doing so. The more we meditate, the deeper we connect with God and our gifts. This is exactly what needs to be happening because you are a lightworker. You are here to bring love and light to the world. Do you recall your hypnosis session? You said you knew why you were born into your family and why you suffered so much. You said it was so that you could learn and heal and then help others heal."

"Yes, I do recall that." I am still unsure how I can be a lightworker though. I am just beginning to work on my gunk."

"Like I mentioned a few months ago, healers are the most wounded and you are no exception but you have such a powerful gift that for lack of a better way to explain it overpowers a lot of your gunk. So, others are drawn to your love and light even when you may feel that your vibrations are low."

"I see. Well, I was hoping for a session today to help me to reset or something."

"Sure, we can do that. We can cleanse you and balance your Chakras and I think it's time you consider taking lightworker training."

"What's that again?"

"It's training on how to connect more deeply with your soul, God, the angels, the Ascended Masters, so you can be of better service for yourself and be of service for others."

"I think that would be great. I need to connect more deeply because I am holding myself back."

"What do you feel you are holding yourself back from?"

"My freedom. It's what the slave told me at Monticello."

"I see. You want to be free of your current life?"

"My life at the Pentagon, yes. I want to be a fulltime writer. After my year in LA, I know this is my path and I know I am scared to death to move out on it."

"Then learning the tools of a lightworker will help you greatly and you can use your gift as a writer to help heal the world."

"I am hopeful it will. I took a Kundalini class a while back. I was hoping it would help and it did but then I just drop back into the fear zone."

"It's time you developed a practice beyond your daily meditation. It's time to learn to tap into your mind, body and soul. You need to understand all parts of you before you can release this fear."

"That makes sense."

"I will be teaching a class in a few weeks. I'll email you more about it and you can decide if you are ready."

"Thank you, Amy."

"You are most welcome. So, are you ready for some energy healing?"

"Yes, I am."

I take off my shoes, hop on the massage table and close my eyes. I feel a deep wave rush over me as Amy stands over me. It's as if my entire body has been swept away and only my soul remains. I am drifting into a trance like my soul has taken over this session. I think I hear Amy speaking to me but I am unable to respond. This is so different than previous times with her. It's like my soul is hungry for this and it's doing work on me as well as Amy. I feel so light and free. Am I levitating? Surely not but I don't dare open my eyes to see. I love this feeling and I am going to float here for as long as possible.

Amy whispers, "I see an eagle pecking at your head. I am asking my Guides for more information and they say you know what this means."

"It's my job." I whisper back.

"Really?"

"Yes. The eagle is used as a symbol for the Air Force."

"I see. Well, this is interesting because your energy is high yet this image is rather frightening. How is work going for you?"

"I'm there, existing waiting to pay back five years for taking the fellowship. I think it's saying my job is an annoyance but I am surviving. But if I don't leave as soon as I can the pecking will drill a hole in me and kill me."

"You are very insightful and definitely ready for lightworker training."

We are both quiet again as Amy continues.

My floating is coming to an end as I feel myself coming back into my body. I feel the weight of me. I feel my body on the table. I hear Amy ask me to sit up and she continues to work on me. I am loose and free and this time she is not having to ask me to relax as she moves my arms and legs. This tells me so much. I want this. I want this easy carefree existence. I want my freedom.

My session comes to an end as Amy passes along messages for me from my spirit guides and Ascended Masters.

"You are supposed to be in California."

"You will return soon and it will be for a great purpose."

"My eyes are barely open as I hear these words and I feel a great sense of comfort."

Perhaps this lightworker training will be what I need to get me going as Amy said. What I know is I owe it to Sally, my ancestors and me to free myself.

Facebook, Oct 29, 2016

Just leaving Debbie Allen's "Freeze Frame". Excellent production! I was moved to tears. We've lost so many lives. There's a role each of us can play to change this path we're on. We can make a difference and lives can be saved. I'm getting in where I fit in to help make a change.

Seeing this musical reminds me of my trip to Monticello. I am free and I don't have the worries that some have. I am not unaware that I am black and can be stopped, assaulted, or killed by the police just because but for the most part this is not a worry I have. I worry for others. I feel a sense of protection in this way like I am safe because my purpose is to support my people and the entire world and since I have yet to start, I am safe from harm.

10
New York

Facebook, Nov 11, 2016

I'm writing *as I head to New York! I decided to take the bus so I could have uninterrupted writing time. We just stopped for a break and I just wrapped up two hours of writing and was flowing like a fountain of literature* 😊

But taking a break to say Happy Veterans Day! Thanks to those who have, do and will someday serve. And a special thanks to my dad who is a veteran who supports my dreams 100%.

I wonder why I wrote that last sentence since it is a lie. My dad doesn't support my dreams. He supports my staying enslaved to my federal career. I need to pray about this. One minute I am using Facebook as social media therapy and the next I'm lying about my life. Part of my healing has got to be to stop making my life seem like a fairytale.

Anyway, I have to thank my terrible date for coming to New York. We met at the salon where I get my crochet braids. He came in to say hello to the women that work there and struck up a conversation with me. In that moment I thought nothing of it as I was sitting there with half my hair in crochet hair and the other half showing my cornrows but afterwards, he stopped me on my way to my car and asked for my number. I figured anyone who could see me looking like that is worth a date and I have to keep getting out here if I want to meet someone.

As for the date, I don't know which part was worse, the friends that were at the restaurant with him or the fact that he tried to convince me to go home with him after dinner. But in all of that he noted he thought I was boring and not a risk taker. He said I should be living my life to the fullest. I kind of thought I was but I am open to other people's perceptions of me. And he wasn't wrong. In just a few months since my return, I've noticed I'm back to my DMV hermit ways. So, here I am in New York. I've lived in the DMV for years and I am just getting here so thank you bad date dude for the encouragement! Plus, it's a two for one trip. I'm treating myself to a trip to new York, for pleasure and to finish up my laser hair removal treatments as New York is the closest location for the company I started with back in Santa Monica. I don't know when he will come into my life but when he does, he will enjoy my smooth underarms and landing strip.

Taking the bus was the best idea and I did write for ninety percent of the ride. As I exit the bus and wait for our bags to be unloaded, I stop to take it all in to include the blistering cold winds. The forecast said it would be in the 60s but I see 60s in New York with the wind whipping through these skyscrapers is quite different than 60s in the DMV.

I see my suitcase and feel the excitement run through my body. The bus dropped us off at Penn Station and I am staying at the Collection Hotel. I have no idea where I am and I am freezing as all I have is a wool blazer and no coat. I try to hail a cab and see this is nothing like the movies. Every cab is zipping by and already has a passenger. I begin to walk and try to hail a cab but still no luck.

I think I'm going to have to walk to my hotel and from what I see on my phone it's only about a 15-minute walk. I look around and see people busily moving down the sidewalk. People brush by me with no regard. It's early, only 2 PM and I feel safe so here we go. I begin walking and picking up my pace as I go. I have a small rolling suitcase and I am careful not to hit anyone with it though I see others with rolling briefcases and suitcases who do not share my concern.

As I make my way to the hotel, I am halted briefly by a Veteran's Day Parade that has Sesame Street characters. I watch and wait then cross the street. I glance down at my phone and see I am making good time and have managed to not get turned around as I have been known to do when using the walking directions. I am careful not to look like I am lost as I don't want to be targeted by muggers but there's not a whole lot I can do but keep moving.

Finally, I arrive at my hotel. I make my way inside and over to the counter to check in.

A young man is grinning from ear to ear.

"Hello and welcome to the Collection Hotel! May I have your name?"

"Ava McClure."

"Yes, Ms. McClure I have your reservation right here. You will be on the foreign language floor."

"Oh, wow okay."

"Yes, in our Asian literature room."

"Thank you."

"The elevator is just down the hall. Please let us know if you need anything during your stay."

"Thanks."

I turn and head down the hall. The elevator is open and I enter. This is going to be a fantastic weekend! I am certain of it. New things for Ava McClure begin now!

I step out of the elevator and walk down the hall. I open the door and to my surprise the room is better than the pictures online. There is not a theme per se but a nicely decorated room in a black and white color scheme. The bathroom is roomy with a huge tub. I look at the books on the shelves that wrap around the room. I pick up one and see it's written in what I believe to be Mandarin. I only know Spanish and very little at that so no reading for me. Next time I will be sure to see if I can request a floor with books I can read.

For now though I have to head back out for my laser appointment. I am a bit sad as the room is nice and toasty and I am just warming up and I will have to deal with this cold again to get to my appointment.

Back in the lobby I ask the bellhop if he could help me hail a cab. He asks, "Where do you need to go?"

"To the Flatiron District."

"No need to waste time and money on a cab, you can just walk. It's only about a 10-minute walk from here."

Oh well then, I guess I should walk. I don't want to though as I know I will be an ice cube again but hey I'm here and I do want to do things the New York way.

"Thank you, I didn't realize it was so close."

"Yes Ma'am. Just head this way down Park Avenue and you can't miss it."

I reach in my pocket and hand him a ten-dollar bill. I have no idea if this is a good amount but it seems fair for directions.

I head outside and start walking. I have my hands in my blazer pockets but the pockets are shallow and my hands are not staying warm. I can't put my hands in my jean pockets because I have my wallet in my front pocket. I don't know if this will keep me from getting mugged but I've heard of people doing it so we'll see.

I'm heading down Park Avenue and feeling more in alignment with the rhythm of the people. Not having my rolling suitcase is also a big help.

I arrive at the laser place and enter.

"Hello! You must be Ava!"

"Yes, I am."

"Great, you're a bit early and Jenny is free so this works out! Please have a seat and she will be right with you."

I take a seat in the ultra-swanky lobby. The royal blue wingback chairs are velvet and as I sit, I rub my hands along the arms of the chair. Yeah, I could get use to this. The location in Santa Monica is nice too and I had a similar feeling each time I came for an appointment but this is New York. For goodness sake I am in Manhattan sitting in a velvet chair, freezing of course because the wind kicked my ass but none the less, I am here. I have been enjoying a rather regal year and a half. From our luxury stay at the Ocean View Resort when we first arrived in Santa Monica to my boutique apartment building out there to living in the richness that is LA life to now here in Manhattan. Biggie and his crew say Mo Money Mo Problems. I say mo money mo enjoyable life. I think you just have to come at it with grace and humility. I don't know but I am determined to find out.

I am so lost in my thoughts I almost jump out of the fancy chair when I see Jenny standing in front of me.

"Hello Ava! I'm ready for you to come back."

"Great, thank you!"

I follow Jenny down the hall and she opens the door. The room is cold, which is no surprise as I have had a few sessions but I was barely warming up and now I will have to get naked and put this terrycloth wrap on for Jenny to zap me up.

She leaves the room and I quickly get undressed and hop on the table.

I hear a soft knock on the door.

"Ready for me?"

"Yes."

Jenny enters with a big grin. She is very pretty. Tall, blonde and maybe 25 at best.

"I see this is your fifth appointment so you know the drill."

"Yes, I am starting to get used to it. Kind of."

"Trust me, I don't know anyone who ever gets used to it! I'll start with your underarms."

She hands me the sunglasses and I put them on and smile. I raise my left arm and she begins. I have a fairly high tolerance for pain so the underarms are a breeze.

"Okay, now for the fun part. So, you know, I have a unique technique. I start on the inside and work my way out. This way the most painful part is over with first."

"Sounds good, thank you."

She smiles and I spread my legs wide. I know the saying beauty is pain but there has to be one that says beauty is no shame because to spread your legs like you are about to enjoy a tongue or a penis but what you are getting is the feeling of burning glass sliding around your vulva requires one to be very comfortable with themselves. I am one of those people. Yep, no shame at all just naked showing my va-jay-jay to a stranger in the middle of the day in Manhattan New York. And Jenny is good. She is going deep and covering every inch down there.

"I see you had your first few sessions in Santa Monica."

"Yes, I lived out there last year for work."

"Must be nice and much warmer."

"It is. I miss it."

"Do you live here now?"

"No, I am just visiting for the weekend. I saw you had a location here and since this is the closest location to where I live in Arlington Virginia, I figured I would have my next session here."

"Smart. I hope you enjoy your time here."

Jenny has just finished. I think they think small talk helps you take your mind off the pain but it doesn't.

"Thank you. Would you be able to tell me how to get to Macy's from here?"

"Oh sure, just head over to 5th Avenue and then to Broadway and then wait you know what. Hold on get dress and I'll be right back."

I hop off the table and get dressed. As I am putting on my shoes Jenny knocks and peeps in.

"Here you go. This should help. It's a map of Manhattan and it has the subway info if you need it."

"Thank you!"

"Sure. I've had this for a while but I don't need it anymore."

"Where are you from?"

"Kansas. Yep, I'm the crazy country chick who wanted to live in the big city."

"I love it! How long have you lived here?"

"Six months now and I love it! You couldn't pay me to leave."

"Thanks again. I was going to go back to my hotel and change before I go see *The Lion King* but I need a coat."

Jenny laughs.

"The wind, right?"

"Right."

"You'll love *The Lion King* and a coat is more important than your outfit. I've been to a few Broadway shows and people dress like whatever. And you look cute already! You'll be dressed better than many just as you are."

"Thanks, that's good to know."

Jenny opens the door and walks with me to the front desk.

"It was great to meet you, Ava. You should come back in six weeks for your next session. The weather will probably be colder but you get to come back to New York."

"That's a great idea. Thank you, Jenny, for everything!"

I wave goodbye and brace for the cold. I open the door, spot 5th Avenue, and begin another walk in the frigid wind.

Everyone is so friendly. I wouldn't have thought that but then again, I've spoken to employees at the hotel and the staff at the laser place all who are in the customer service industry so it makes sense.

I move quickly down Broadway and as I do I see entrances for the subway. I am curious to just walk down and see one of the stations but that will have to wait. The sun is beginning to set and the temperature is dropping. I look up and see 34th Street and there it is, Macy's! The Macy's I have heard about my entire life. The Macy's I knew I would shop at frequently when I planned to be a big fashion designer when I was a teenager. The Macy's that sponsors the Thanksgiving Day Parade.

I cross the street and brace myself as I enter. To my surprise I am in a Winter Wonderland. There is so much holiday'ness happening I am unable to focus. Every inch of the store is decorated in Christmas delight. Music is playing and people everywhere.

Okay, Ava. Focus. You need a coat and you need to be mindful of the time as the show starts at 8 PM. I look around for signs to point me in the direction of women's apparel or something along those lines but I don't see any so I decide to take the escalator up and just start looking. How many floors is this place? I seem to keep going and going and now I am riding an old rickety though I am sure they would call it vintage or something escalator and have landed on the top floor. I get off and take a quick look around and find a salesperson.

"Hello, can you point me in the direction of women's coats?"

"Yes, third floor."

"Thank you."

I find my way to the down escalator and get off on the third floor. To my amusement and horror, I am looking at a sea of coats. Never in my life have I seen these many coats all in one location. It appears this entire floor is full of women's coats. Where to start? I walk around for a bit and notice that they are labeled based on departments - women's, juniors, petite. I quickly make my way to the petite section which still has probably a thousand coats. How in the world am I supposed to select a coat when everything here is so beautiful? I finally land on a charcoal gray coat that is more of a wrap with a sash. I try it on and it fits perfectly over my thick wool blazer so it is clearly the coat for me.

I look around for the checkout counter and finally find it. I am happy no one is in line as I walk up.

The sales lady rings me up and I pull out my credit card to pay. She begins to pull out the long plastic bag for my coat and I stop her.

"Excuse me. Do you have scissors?"

"Hum let me check. Ah yes, I do."

"Thank you. Would you mind if we cut the tags off? I'd like to wear it now."

"She glances me over and notices my blazer and smiles."

"Of course! You must be freezing!"

"Yes, I wasn't expecting it to be this cold. I'm from Virginia."

"It's the Hudson River. It makes it unbearably cold and because of the height of the buildings the sun never warms anything up and now it's dark outside so you most definitely need to be wearing this."

"She cuts the tags off and hands me my receipt and the tags."

I thank her as I slip on the coat and search for the escalator.

Man, what a day! Up early. On a bus for four hours. Dropped off somewhere in Manhattan. Found my way to my hotel. Walked down several famous streets and bought my first item and souvenir from Macy's! And my day is not done as I have a ticket to see *The Lion King* in a few hours.

I check my watch and see it's just 5:30 PM. I have time to go back to the hotel but I would be starving all night as I won't have time to go back to the hotel, change and get something to eat. Food wins and Jenny did say I was dressed well enough. I'm guessing it's like going to the Kennedy Center. Some go all out and dress up and others show up in jeans. It's just fancy to me because this is my first Broadway show.

I pull out the map Jenny gave me and see which way I need to head. Surely there will be places to eat as I head to Times Square. For the first time since I arrived, I am excited to go outside and walk. My new coat is nice and toasty and it is quite stylish. I pass a few restaurants but none catch my eye until I get to the Hard Rock Café. It seems only fitting that I dine here. I have not been to many of their locations, just Atlantic City, Philly and oh yeah, the one in D.C. I make my way in and take a quick loop around the store. I am mindful of the time so I follow the signs to the restaurant. To my surprise the line has about 30 people in it. I don't think I can wait this long as I will miss the show. Looks like I could have gone back and changed. At least I would've gotten to wear my cute little black dress and be hungry now I'll just be hungry.

"Hello everyone!"

I turn to see the host.

"We want to let you know there is going to be an hour and a half wait minimum tonight but if you are okay sitting at the bar there is immediate seating."

I waste no time and walk up to him. I see I am the only one.

"Hello ma'am, please come in."

He opens the door and I enter. This Hard Rock Café is enormous. It's almost as overwhelming as Macy's. I see the bar straight ahead and make my way there. I opt for a seat that is close to one of the televisions which is playing music videos. The bartender comes over with a menu.

"How are you tonight?"

"Great, thank you."

"What can I get you to drink?"

"A glass of Riesling, thank you."

"Coming up."

I open the menu and look for the burgers. I haven't eaten all day and I am now awakening to the fact that I'm starving.

"Anything look good?"

"Yes, the bacon cheeseburger."

"How would you like it?"

"Well done, thank you."

"I'll put that in for you."

I focus my attention on the television which is playing *Ain't It Funny*. It feels as though I have never seen this video and I watch with intrigue. J. Lo and Ja Rule in the early 2000s. Life was good back then. Or was it? I was dating the best man I'd ever known but thought he was too good for me so I broke up with him and started back dating someone who was not the second best or even third best man I'd known. I wonder if I had of thought about therapy then would I have kept dating that wonderful man instead of ending things just a few months after we met. Oh well, no need in thinking of it as the past is the past.

The bartender brings my food and a bottle of ketchup for my fries. I cut the burger in half and take a bite. I am in heaven. I take a sip of my wine and a deep breath. This weekend is just what I needed. My job sucks and my pod/table mate Ted is a pain in the ass. He wants to do his job and my job and all the while doesn't know anything. But yet this is what we do. Hire back the military and make them double dippers.

I want this weekend to be a cleanse or reset or something. I have resolved I need to be in the DMV for things I have yet to discover but I don't think it means I have to keep working for the government. My trip to Monticello was a wakeup call that I am indeed enslaving myself. No one is holding me at Shawshank but me.

I realize I've digressed in my thoughts. I flag the bartender and ask for my check. I pay and head out. Back in the Hardrock store I pull out my trusty map and see I am just a few blocks away from the theater.

11

Times Square

Times Square! I'm here! I am not sure what I am supposed to do but be here and take it all in. The bright lights and the people and those dressed in dirty costumes reminds me of the Batman I saw when I first arrived in Santa Monica last year. I find the theater as I pass several others and gawk at marquees. Shows I've heard of and I am passing their respective theaters.

I pick up my ticket from Will Call and still have thirty minutes before they open for entry. I take a look around and see a souvenir store. Cleo and Sophie! Oh, please let them have some cute dog items. I walk to the store and much like Macy's and the Hard Rock Café I am overwhelmed. Stuff everywhere. I take a deep breath and scan the store. I spot an area for pets and walk that way. To my delight they have so many things that neither Cleo nor Sophie would want but I think are adorable. Ski puffer jackets that say I Heart NY, hoodies, and t-shirts. I pick one of each for the girls and then see the squeaky toys. Two pink dog bones that say I Heart NY something they will actually love and I'm done.

As I walk back to the theater I think of the girls. I miss them but I know it's important for me to take this break. Before entering I walked around 46th street and read the show titles. As I round the block back to 45th street I claim it. My novel will be adapted into a Broadway show and it will be a hit! It will be critically acclaimed and win Tony Awards! Amen! It occurred to me while watching Debbie Allen's

Freeze Frame at the Kennedy Center the other week that my work could be converted into a Broadway production. Of course, first I must write the novel and yes ma'am Sally I am now putting my heart into it!

I walk up to the theater and see a line has formed. I take my place in line and check out those around me. Some are dressed up and some are in jeans. The usher walks down to greet us and makes an announcement.

"Please be sure to look at your seat numbers. This will help everyone to get seated quickly. Thank you."

I take a look at my ticket. I splurged and got a seat up close. I am in row H. As I make my way inside the theater I try to take it all in. Posters of *The Lion King,* the red carpet lining the halls, the gold walls.

An usher shows me to my seat and I settle in taking my coat off and placing my bag of souvenirs on the floor under my seat. My row quickly fills up and the lights dim.

I hear voices projected from the back of the theater and as they get louder, I see a magnificent parade of characters seemingly gliding down the aisle and onto the stage. I had been told by one of my coworkers that I would be taken away and that after a few moments I would forget that I was looking at humans and would fall deeply into only seeing the characters. These costumes are breathtaking and I am in awe. I am sitting in a Broadway theater on a Friday night watching

The Lion King!

The show ends with thunderous applause and a message noting the actors will be available for pictures and discussion immediately afterwards. I glance at my watch and see it is 10:30 PM. I am feeling the urge to pee so I find the restroom and wait in line.

As I exit the restroom and go around the corner, I see some of the actors. I would love to stop and speak with them but I am getting nervous. I have walked to every destination today and I think I should continue this mode of transportation instead of attempting to hail a cab in Times Square. I have felt very comfortable and safe all day but now it's getting late and the streets may not be as full of residents and tourists as I get closer to the hotel so I'd better hurry along.

As I leave the theater I stop and turn back to take it in. Yep, I did it. All by myself, which I must admit is nice to say but also lonely. I long for the day I can take trips with my man. I am confident the day will come but tonight I am solo. I chuckle as I recall my Ode to Stedman Graham, I made up years ago.

Oh, where oh where is my Stedman at? Oh, where oh where could he be? With his independent life and his love for me oh where oh where could he be?

Is it wrong to want my own version of Stedman? For the past 30 years or so I have watched Oprah and Stedman and it seems like a pretty nice deal to me; not too much not too little just enough of the right amount of time with each other.

A while back Shonda Rhimes was on Oprah's *Super Soul Sunday* show. Of everything they discussed, all I remember is Shonda saying she didn't want to be married, she just wanted a boyfriend. I am probably totally jacking up what she actually said but the point is we are monogamous but you are not always in my house.

I want the man who loves me, adores me and thinks the world of me as I do of him. I just don't want him in my space all the time. I want to travel and take trips. I want us to be exclusive of course but I'm not so sure about the whole marriage thing. Though there are days when I watch too many movies on the Hallmark Channel and I begin thinking I'm lying to myself and I really do want that life. You know, husband, the kids, the house and picket fence. I don't really know what I want but I could start off with a Stedman. I think I have allowed myself to believe I'm supposed to want more because that's what people think you should have. For now, I will continue to walk back to the hotel alone and stay hopeful. He's out there and he and I will meet someday soon.

It's meditation. The more I meditate the more confident I feel. There's a knowing that I am worthy and deserving of the life I desire. It's more than relaxing it's life altering. I wish my girlfriends could get this but I am just happy they don't give me any pushback well except Sheryl. We've barely spoken since I allowed by beautifully balanced Solar Plexus Chakra to fill me and speak up for myself at Happy Hour.

I walk through Times Square and hold a visual of the map in my mind as I have no intentions of taking it out or my phone this late at night to draw attention to myself. To my surprise the streets are still full of activity. I guess I shouldn't be surprised as this is New York. What's that saying or is it a song? The city that never sleeps. I think that's a song. Anyway I feel good though I notice my pace is much faster than earlier. Before I was moving with the rhythm of the streets, now I am moving to hurry up and go to bed. It's been a long day and also a day I will never forget.

I open the door to my hotel room and place the bag of souvenirs on the armchair. I walk into the bathroom and smile at the bathtub. I am always delighted when hotel rooms have bathtubs so I can continue my nightly ritual. I slowly get undressed as the water fills the tub. I begin thinking, what's stopping me from having this? And by this, I mean this kind of life. The life that allows me to enjoy time in New York, take in a Broadway show and stay in a luxurious boutique hotel. Living the life of a federal employee will only get this type a living once in a while and I want this every day. I've noticed I have been thinking about money and the rich life a lot lately. Maybe it's my LA hangover. But it's not the money and the lifestyle itself, it's the freedom from federal service that I desire. And, if I am in my purpose, writing will yield financial abundance and there is nothing wrong with having a nice life. I see it as a beautiful energy exchange.

And yes, there will be stuff to deal with in my wonderful writing world. I am a firm believer that there is crazy everywhere and I am certain I will find it in the publishing industry, film industry and on Broadway. But at least I will be doing what I am supposed to be doing not trying to stay afloat in the stormy waters of this Air Force bureaucracy.

I slide into the tub and let my thoughts go. I managed to get in a good meditation on the bus ride this morning and now this hot bath will be my transcendence into a good night's sleep.

12
Not Like Sex and the City

I am in the New York Public Library! This space is beautiful and there are tourists everywhere even in the reading and study rooms. I am recalling the scene from the movie *Sex and the City* where Carrie returns library books and discovers the upstairs as the place for her and Big's wedding. Ah the movies! Nothing like reality. The books are across the street in a nondescript building and thinking more about that scene, doesn't she give the books to the security guard? Kind of odd now that I think about it.

I was thinking I would do some writing here today and Zen on the good vibes filling this magnificent structure. And I can. I can write with tourists all around. I can be creative in a not so quiet space. I can because I get wrapped in my work. I take another look around and feel the smile on my face as I take a seat in one of the reading rooms. As I begin to type on my tablet I feel my heart flutter. To know a part of my first novel will have been written in this space brings a sense of fulfillment to my spirit.

Before exploring and finding my way into this room I bought a magnet from the gift shop that has a quote from George Elliot, "It's never too late to be what you might have been." It's the first thing my eyes focused on when I entered the gift shop. I know I have time to be a published author of books, film, Broadway etc. As my spin class instructor used to say there's no one standing in my way but me. And

Sally gave me a good kick in the butt not too long ago with this same message.

Now, I write.

I am leaving the library and heading down the street to visit the Empire State Building. As I begin walking, I hear shouting. I now see a crowd of people with signs. I continue walking as they approach. They are protesting the results of the election. It was a shocker to the world. I watched the election results until midnight then awoke to a new president. A parade yesterday, a protest today. I know there's going to be some mega dark energy after he is sworn in. This last year was flooded with some interesting candidates all with an agenda but none whose agenda seem to serve the United States just themselves so the way I see it anyone of them was a bad pick. And this will certainly open the flood gates for all kinds of characters to run for president next term.

I watch for a few more minutes before continuing to the Empire State Building.

Facebook, Nov 12, 2016

Fitness Challenge!!! Take 6 flights of stairs or wait 25 minutes to take the elevator up to the observatory floor. I'm happy to say I took the stairs 😄

I'm glad I was able to visit the Empire State Building today. Making it all the way to the very top, which is the observatory floor felt special. It was the tiniest space and a bit claustrophobic but worth the extra few bucks I paid to see the view from there.

As the sun sets, I decide to forgo my hop on hop off night bus tour and look for a restaurant. I am getting the hang of Midtown. It's like a big square which makes it easy to navigate. Tomorrow, I venture to Central Park before I head back home. This weekend was needed and I am happy I came as I know when I return there will be work to do and not just at Shawshank. I've decided to take Amy's lightworker class. It's time I deepened my practice so I can finally get those answers I've been longing to hear from God or maybe they are already in me. I am beginning to believe it's the latter. That's what Marva would say. My purpose is part of my soul contract with God so my soul already knows. Well, soul I am ready to reconnect with you and execute my soul contract.

Facebook, Nov 12, 2016

A little complementary wine and cheese to close out my day. When asked Red, White or Prosecco I opted for the latter. A little bubbly to celebrate my life. I'm blessed and so thankful that I can live a wonderful life and do whatever my heart desires, be it travel or becoming a successful writer. God has equipped me to live a boundless life!

Facebook, Nov 13, 2016

What a great weekend! From my first Broadway show, The Lion King which was amazing to beautiful Central Park I am truly blessed to have had the opportunity to spend time in New York. I really haven't taken advantage of the fact that I can go and do whatever I want pretty much whenever I want. But the light did finally come on this weekend. I have no excuses not to live it up!

13
Lightworker Training

It's 7 PM and I am at a yoga studio in Bethesda Maryland. I am sitting on the floor next to two other women as we watch Amy arrange yoga mats and blankets on the floor. I am not sure what will happen over the next two and a half days but I'm ready.

The two women are Nancy and Pam. They seem just as unsure as I am about what will be going on but just as eager to get to a deeper level of soul connection.

"Ladies, thank you for joining me today."

Amy, as always is speaking softly and has her angelic smile.

"This weekend will be an opportunity for you to learn several practices that will support you in knowing yourself more and in doing so connect you deeply with your soul. You will be able to use this deep connection to be of service to others. You are blessed as healers and this is your first step in living out your purpose.

We smile and thank Amy.

The night ends with some somatic exercises to help us transition into our lives at home. While tonight's class was only two hours it was quite challenging. Many of the exercises we learned were about centering and focus – being fully present. It was challenging for me because I am always lost in my thoughts. Sure, I can be quiet and let my thoughts go during my meditations but to do something like focus my attention on a particular area on the wall was a completely different experience. I now see why having a mantra is helpful for meditation. Sitting quietly is an open invitation to let my mind go full steam ahead with some digression here and there.

I slept well last night and I am ready for day two of class. Amy begins.

"The first thing we will learn is a breathing technique called Nadi Shodhana or alternate nostril breathing. It helps to balance the left and right side of the brain. And you can activate your left or right brain by inhaling with the opposite nostril."

I watch as Amy demonstrates and I am floored. I took a Kundalini class in Santa Monica but didn't learn this. Actually, it was more of a Heart Chakra Gong Healing ceremony but we did do some Kundalini exercises and breathwork just not this technique. Of course, it was one event and there are hundreds of practices around the globe. I shouldn't be shocked I am just learning of this one but I am floored. I have to bite my lip to keep from laughing as Amy finishes her demonstration. You are shitting me, right? All I had to do was this? Had I known this two years ago I wouldn't have this device in my head. This device that could be slowly rotting out my brain and killing me. I could have just switched from left brain to right brain with breathwork!

It's now our turn to practice and I allow myself to focus and slowly do the breathwork. I am feeling the balance and I am feeling the shift as I only focus on inhaling through my right nostril. That left brain'ish feeling is starting to surface. Well God all I can say you got me good! But it was me so desperate for change that I allowed

Monique to operate on my brain. I pray I am well and will never have brain damage from this thing.

Amy said she will be teaching Reiki Level I next month and I plan to take the class. I feel I need to learn as much as I can to help myself heal. I have been back for several months and I have not checked in with Dr. Smith. I don't feel the need to as I feel so much more lifted than I ever did in therapy. I am seeing what Amy was saying during my Reiki session. I am light years away from where I was last fall even with the darkness of the DMV around me.

Facebook, Nov 16, 2016

iana Ross performing with the NSO at the Kennedy Center. Love her!!! Got my ticket! My Christmas present to me from me with love

Oh yes! I am a Diana Ross fan for life! My seat is in the orchestra section so I will be close and can take in all of her essence. There was only one seat left so I'm going solo. I could have sacrificed and sat somewhere else but nope I've got to be as close as possible. Marva and I saw her a few years ago at the Artistic Pavilion and our seats were so high up Ms. Ross looked like at dot on the stage. I am not sure when I first knew of Diana but it's been a one-sided love affair since I was about eight years old. I remember watching *Mahogany* and *Lady Sings the Blues* long before I probably should have and was glued to the television during her television specials. Whenever I'd get in trouble I would daydream of Diana and Billy Dee Williams. They after all had to be my real parents and any day now, they were coming to take me home. Of course, it never happened and Tracee Ellis Ross is only four months older than me but it didn't stop me from dreaming. It's interesting all those times I saw her youngest daughter at the coffee shop in Santa Monica I never once spoke. I just couldn't. I didn't want her to think I was speaking to her because she was Diana Ross' daughter, I truly wanted to introduce myself because she owned the children's bookstore up the street but it doesn't matter now. What matters is on December 3rd it will be Ms. Ross and me.

14
Soul to Soul

Last night I had the most interesting dream. I was sitting in a dark room with Diana Ross and she told me everything I ever wanted will come to be in the next one to two years. That's it. That's all she said. I said okay and now I'm awake and thinking how freaking wonderful! I will be a successful author able to make a living as a writer. But I want more than that. I want love. I've been praying and meditating with my rose quartz. Praying to be open to giving and receiving love. Surely, she meant that aspect of my life too since she did say everything I've ever wanted. I can't wait to see how the next one to two years unfolds.

I also need to call Monique. This device has been broken for over a year. I was happy with it not functioning and even being back at Shawshank is not a motivating factor in getting it fixed. My meditations, breathwork and the new exercises I learned in lightworker training the other week are more than enough. I can handle the perpetual Groundhog Days without shifting into left brain robotic Ava. I can manage my life and my approach with others using these practices. But I should at least have her check things out. I'll give her a call soon.

15
Meeting Mr. Sexy

Facebook, Dec 3, 2016

Post – *don't fear failure fear being in the exact same place you are today.*

Perfect post for a perfect night! Ms. Ross had to have this belief to enjoy such a successful career. And Ms. Sally didn't say this when she came to me at Monticello but I think she would agree.

I'm dressed in my cobalt blue summer dress though it's freezing here in the DMV. My hair has transformed into waist length wavy crimped crochet braids. There is something about Diana Ross, her grace, her elegance, her charm, and her ability to seemingly float across the stage that has always captivated me.

Tonight is extra special because of the dream I had the other night. I have been daydreaming about the one to two years. What if it means not only am I heading back to California but in the next year or two my novel about Shawshank will be a number one bestseller and a blockbuster movie!

As I pull up to the Kennedy Center fond memories drift into my thoughts. My friends and I have spent many nights here enjoying performances from the Alvin Ailey Dance Theater to the Nutcracker ballet. I recall coming here one night and eating across the street at

The Watergate Hotel many years ago with my friends. It was an interesting place, and we were the only brown spots in the restaurant. Rich older white people come to The Watergate Hotel for dinner is what I gathered after looking around, but it didn't matter as it was my first time at the Kennedy Center to see The Nutcracker and I wasn't going to let the air of whiteness ruin the evening. Here I am eight years later rolling solo. I feel not one ounce of guilt for not inviting my friends. For starters I was not going to give up sitting so close to Ms. Ross to sit in tiers I or II and my crew is on some extreme CP (colored people's) time.

I exit my car and head up to Will Call. I'm feeling quite fabulous and sexy. This dress is turning heads not to mention my waist length locks bouncing as I walk.

I am relieved the line at Will Call is fairly short. I'm here early so there's no rush just me and time but I would like to walk around and take in the essence of being here as the beauty of this building never gets old.

Out of the corner of my eye I see a man and my body turns to face him. I say body because it feels like it reacted before my brain did. He is quite handsome. Tall, golden wavy hair, and chiseled. He is wearing a black suit, with a slender gray tie. I smile in delight of his presence, and he winks and smiles back. If feels like we're smiling and staring at each other for hours. I notice the person in front of me move. I shake my head and move to the next window.

"Hello ma'am. May I help you?"

"Yes, thank you. Ava McClure.

"Here's your ticket. Enjoy the show."

"Thank you very much."

I am beaming on the inside! I can't believe I'm going to see Diana Ross perform with the National Symphony Orchestra! Her voice with an orchestra, what more could anyone ask for?

As I leave Will Call, there he is again walking by only this time as he passes we are only about two feet apart. He turns, stops, and stares at me and I feel a rush of energy as if there's this force flowing between his body and mine. I'm drawn to him. It is magnetizing.

"Hello. I must say that you are the most beautiful woman I've ever seen!"

"Thank you."

I think I am smiling but I might be standing here with my mouth wide open and gazing.

"My name is Lucas."

Do I detect a Latin accent?

"I'm Ava."

"What brings you here tonight?"

"I'm here to see Diana Ross."

"Ah that's wonderful! I'm here to meet a business partner and his wife. There is a ballet in the Opera House tonight."

"Yes, I heard about that but between Diana Ross and the ballet I had to choose Diana Ross."

Lucas laughs, "I don't blame you! I would have chosen Diana Ross too, but this is a business thing."

"Of course."

I smile back. I can't take my eyes off of this man. His piercing blue eyes are rather hypnotizing.

"Would it be **okay if I give** you my number?"

I'm remembering the movie *He's Just Not That Into You*. What's the rule? If he gives you his number, he's not that into you?

"You can **or** I could give you my number."

I think this is how it's supposed to go. I am having a hard time remembering the movie right now.

"Oh, of course. **I didn't want to seem too forward, but I will** certainly take your number!"

He hands me his phone and I put my number in. I hand it back and he smiles.

"I hope you have a wonderful **evening, Ava.**"

"You too Lucas. **It was nice meeting you.**"

We part ways and I head to the Concert Hall. The doors haven't opened yet and the line is wrapped around the corner but it's a fun experience as I am chatting with an older couple in front of me though I must admit these Ivanka Trump shoes I'm wearing while cute as heck are taking my feet to new levels of pain. But I've got to hand it to her she managed to make the perfect nude color heel that matches my complexion perfectly.

As the doors open and the crowd begins to move forward, I see my phone light up in my purse. I pull it out and see it is a text from Lucas:

It was really nice meeting you Ava. I look forward to speaking with you tomorrow.

I reply:

It was nice meeting you too. I am looking forward to chatting as well.

It appears Lucus is into me. We'll see how things go tomorrow. Returning to the DMV and being free and clear of Dan has made for a nice transition back. Maybe Lucas is the reason I'm back and my investigative journalism of Shawshank for my novel of course. Meeting a sexy Latino man at the Kennedy Center and I've only been back a couple of months, I think that's a pretty nice start to life back on the East Coast!

Facebook, Dec 3, 2016

So...I'm waiting in the Will Call line when this very handsome man winks at me . On my way out of the line we meet again and he asks for my number. We exchange numbers and after a few moments of parting ways again he sends me a cute text and...well that's it for now. Cause it's almost time for...Ms. Ross!!!!

Facebook, Dec 3, 2016

So, you know I was done when they said we could take pictures! I was 11 rows away from the stage so you know I was in Diana Heaven

I don't know if it was just me but every song Diana Ross sang tonight seemed to have a special message in it just for me. The lyrics seemed to change ever so slightly to specifically fit me. Then at the end of her show she looked right at me and said, "I see you". For a brief moment our eyes locked and all I could do was nod and whisper, "okay". Then seeming a little confused about it herself she looked away and said, "I see all of you" and begin to thank us for our support. I have no idea if this is how she ends every show but I feel as though tonight it was confirmation of our soul to soul moment in my dream.

I am in my car waiting in line to exit the Kennedy Center and Lucas' text appears.

I hope you enjoyed Diana Ross!

I smile but don't reply. Instead, I slowly creep up in the line and reflect on the moment I first saw him. Could Lucas be my Stedman? Can it be that he will be my last stop on the dating train? A girl can hope since this girl is not a fan of the dating scene especially after Hookah Man and Mr. Come Home with Me.

Facebook, Dec 7, 2016

Updated cover photo: My first Christmas photo.

I was eleven months old for my first Christmas. I think I posted this picture as a reminder to watch out for all those little Ava's. Lucas, the guy I met the night of the concert seems too good to be true. A six-foot-tall sexy man from Argentina. Tall, tan and sexy with blonde wavy hair that brushes the back of his neck. His blue eyes and his accent makes me want to strip my clothes off and let him take me to bed. We've yet to have our first date, just brief conversations on the phone. It is because of his sexy nature and the fact that we have so much in common that I can feel the walls going up. I don't want to start off this way with him but I know I need to protect the little Ava's. I just need to be mindful of what's occurring. I want to be fully open to getting to know him and be open to giving and receiving love as I have been praying and meditating on and I know I cannot have what I truly want if I start putting walls up.

I must admit while I still hate Shawshank, I absolutely adore my new cellmates! Ted can be a bit much sometimes but the rest of the guys and I literally mean men as I am the only female on this side of the office are such a blast to chat it up with. I am reading through an aircraft maintenance policy letter when I decide to turn around and poll the group on Lucas.

"Hey y'all so you know I met the guy at the Kennedy Center last week."

Mike, who sits across the makeshift aisle from me at another two-person table/cubicle arrangement is the first to whirl around in his chair.

"Yeah, so how's that going?"

"We've had a few phone conversations and so far, so good. He wants to take me to dinner tomorrow."

"Okay, progress. Where are you going?"

"That's the thing. I don't know. He hasn't followed up since we spoke a couple of days ago."

"Maybe he's not tracking to the days of the week", says Ted.

"I can easily be off by a day or two sometimes. Just give him a call or text and check in with him."

"Yeah, I should. I just didn't want to seem pushy or anxious."

Brian chimes in.

"That's not pushy. That's letting him know you are not going to sit around and jump at the last minute. You don't want to start off setting a precedent."

"He's right," says Mike. "Don't give us guys any room to make assumptions."

"True," I say.

I should text him.

"Yeah," they all say in unison.

I get up and walk out the office grabbing my cellphone from the locker. I walk down the hall turning on my phone and take a right on the E-Ring. No reception as I suspected. I head down the escalators by the food court and make my way out to the courtyard. I stop just shy of the doors that lead outside as today is an exceptionally cold day and we are in the midst of an ice storm. Not one bad enough to shut down the government for the day but one that says I have no business bebopping out to the courtyard and four-inch heels with ice on the ground.

I check my phone again and see that I have cell service and begin to text.

Hello! I hope your day is going well! Just checking to see if we are still on for tomorrow?

I wait about 30 seconds and check my phone but there is no reply. I am not shocked as Lucas is a surgeon and I'm sure is doing whatever surgeons do during the day. I turn to head back to the office as standing in the breezeway it's proving to be just as cold as probably standing in the courtyard. Since I'm out I might as well treat myself to an afternoon coffee so I walk into the food court.

Standing in line I reflect on what the guys said and they are absolutely correct. I can't help but think perhaps I set some kind of precedent with Dan, something that let him know that I was someone who could not be taken seriously. I most certainly started off on the right foot with Hookah Man and Mr. Come Home with Me.

I am enjoying Lucas and our conversations and I would love to see where this could possibly go though, I must admit I can't see myself long term with someone outside of my race albeit I have dated outside of my race in the past. I guess I always thought when it came to settling down, I would be with a black man but I'm starting to have an open mind about that as well. I was such a rebel of sorts growing up and I still love my blackness though I don't shout it from the rooftops like I once did. That feisty Ava who in the 4th grade decided to stop saying the Pledge of Allegiance because she didn't like the part that said one nation under God and justice for all because as she explained to her teacher this wasn't the case for her people so she didn't believe she needed to pledge to something that isn't true. I recall my teacher looking at me with a faint smile and saying, "okay Ava" and walking away. Anyway, that Ava, the teenage fight the power Ava and the HBCU grad Ava… nope they would never have dated white men and now a Latino. Though in the 4th grade my best friend was white and so was my best friend in high school. And, I love all people but there is something about a strong black man that turns me on. At least the idea of him hence my Ode to Stedman.

Dating outside of my race was never an issue as far as the relationships themselves other than the typical cultural differences but I did get a lot of backlash from black men in Oklahoma when they saw me with a white man. Perhaps here in the DMV dating a Latino will go unnoticed but he is not a brown skinned brunette Latino he is a blonde-haired blue-eyed Latino. Why do I feel like I am talking myself out of this?

I place my order, my usual vanilla latte and smile. Nope Oprah I'm still not ready for that big change but I am going to take a baby step and try the Latin man flavor.

As I wait on my order, I see Dana.

"Hey Ava!"

"Dana!"

"What's up, girl?"

"Not much. Just need an afternoon pick me up."

"Um hum."

Dana is eyeing my phone.

"Who you calling? Mr. Sexy?"

"I just sent him a text message about our date tomorrow. I haven't heard from him and wanted to see if we were still on."

"Oh, you still on."

"How do you know?"

"Cause y'all been talking on the phone and you said you two have a lot in common."

"And?"

"And it's rough out in these streets. That man knows you are an attractive woman with a bomb career. Of course, he doesn't know you hate it but it sounds bomb. You manage billions of dollars for the Air Force. You did tell him that right?"

"No. Why would I tell him that?"

"Girl, to impress his ass. He's a surgeon Ava!"

"So?"

"So, they can date other surgeons, lawyers. Hell, anybody."

"I am somebody. Isn't that what you just said?"

"Yes, when I thought you laid out why the hell you were somebody."

"Seriously Dana? Edward fell for Vivian and she didn't have anything."

"Who?"

"*Pretty Woman*"

"Ava, sweetie, we are not living in some white man's Hollywood bubble okay. But yeah, I guess if all he knows is you's a good ol' government employee and he still wants to take you out then he's your Richard Gere or whatever his name was in that movie."

"Thank you."

I give Dana a half smile as I hear my name called for my latte.

"You know I once dated a man who was amazing. I thought he was too good for me and I ended the relationship. I later found out he married a woman who worked at the mall."

"Okay. Have your *Pretty Woman* fantasy for now but by the end of dinner tomorrow Lucas best know your business. How you be running shit up in this joint."

"Right. Well, I've got to get back to the office but thanks for the pep talk."

"That wasn't a pep talk, that was sage advice. **And d**on't forget those were white folks in *Pretty Woman.* That ain't y'all by a long shot."

Dana is trying to look serious but breaks into laughter.

I roll my eyes and we hug goodbye.

Back in the office, the guys are pleased with my text and assure me Lucas will respond.

"Lead him in the way you want him to go now or complain about him forever," says Brian. The other two nod in agreement.

I am taking the metro to Pentagon City since the ground is still icy. The ride is only a couple of minutes but will spare me any unnecessary slip and falls. As I exit the train, I feel my phone vibrate in my bag. I reach in to pull it out and see I have a text message from Lucas.

Hey! Of course we are still on! This is the highlight of my week 😊

How does 8 at Primo Italiano sound?

I text back.

Wonderful, sounds great!

This will be the highlight of my week too ☺

16
Primo Italiano

I am dressed in a brick red short sleeve dress that is hugging my body. It's fitting but not trashy. I am doing a few rounds of deep belly breathing as I sit in my car. I am ten minutes early for my date with Lucas. We are meeting at an Italian restaurant in Vienna. Alright Ava, you can do this. First you are at a high-priced restaurant, not Casual Days or a hookah club. Second, Lucas is fun to talk to, engaging with his conversations and he is sexy as hell. And hey you've never dated a Latino before so there's that.

I open the car door and slowly get out. It's bitter cold and while I have on a coat, I am barelegged with peep toe patent leather pumps and we are still thawing out from yesterday's winter storm so I am tiptoeing to the entrance.

I enter into a breathtaking ambience. I feel as though I have just walked in off the streets of Italy. The aroma is awakening my stomach. My hunger pains vanish at the sight of Lucas. It's as if he appeared from nowhere.

"Hello, my lovely lady! It is so wonderful to see you again!"

"You too!"

Lucas leans over and gives me a hug and kiss on the cheek.

"Shall we?"

He extends his hand and I take hold of it.

"My godfather owns this restaurant and he has made this evening very special for us."

As we walk through the restaurant, I see people taking notice of us. I guess we look rather intriguing. A tall handsome Latino blonde man with a petite black woman whose hair is reminiscent of Lisa Bonet during her later *Cosby Show* years. Lucas is dressed in black slacks, a cream turtleneck and why this is turning me on I don't know but the way his belt is just ever so slightly fitted around his waist is titillating.

We are now at the back of the restaurant and it looks as though we just stepped outside of our villa onto our patio. The noise of the restaurant has faded and the only sound I hear is my heart beating faster than usual. Lucas walks up to the small round table and pulls out my chair.

"Thank you."

I smile as I sit down with my clutch in my lap.

Lucas waves for the waiter as he takes a seat. The waiter hands us menus then pours water in our glasses.

"May I share tonight's specials with you?"

Lucas seems confused.

"No, we have a special menu planned for tonight."

"Oh, yes of course. My apologies. What can I get you to drink?

I begin to peruse the back of the menu and as I do Lucas speaks.

"We will have a bottle of Chianti."

He smiles at me and I give a faint smile.

"Will do Sir."

I feel like I am having a Dan flashback. I should let Lucas know I am not a fan of red wine.

"Actually, red wine gives me a terrible headache."

"Oh, no we can't have that. Let's make that Chardonnay?"

Lucas gives me a wink and I smile. I am so thankful I spoke up. I can't go through another round of red wine lies.

The waiter nods and walks off.

"So red wine gives you a headache?"

"Yes, I guess I'll never get to truly experience the joy many people have for it."

"Ah well, you're not missing much. So how was your day?"

I hear Dana from yesterday, "Have your Pretty Woman fantasy for now but by the end of dinner tomorrow Lucas best know your business."

"It was good. Nothing exciting."

"Really? I would think working in the Pentagon would be nonstop action."

"No, there's too much bureaucratic tape for that."

"I see."

"I spend my days overseeing the Air Force's Flying hour program which is an important component of the mission."

"Really how so?"

"It's the flightline maintenance and fuel cost associated with our various fleets."

I decide to keep it simple. No need and no one cares about all the moving parts of the program.

"So how was your day?"

"Pretty boring too. Just removed a benign tumor from a two-year old's brain."

"Sure, I can see where that's boring."

I give a sarcastic smirk.

He laughs.

"Actually, it is in a way. I mean it's wonderful to help people as a surgeon but being a neurosurgeon comes with a cost."

"How so?"

"Like the night we met. I was entertaining some potential donors for the hospital. Our chief of surgery likes to send me to shmooze with the rich folks because neuro is a fascinating subject to many people. Just once I'd liked to be overlooked and have one of our general surgeons go and chat them up about hernia repairs."

"Well, having had a hernia repair I would be interested in that chat."

"Really? How long ago?"

"About seven or eight years ago."

Lucas reaches over and runs his finger down my stomach.

"I hope it healed well and no issues since."

The mere sliding of his finger down my dress makes me shiver. I'm already hanging on to every word he says. I am a sucker for a sexy accent.

"Um yes it healed just fine and I was back to working out in no time."

"Good. I can see you take working out seriously."

I think I'm blushing.

"I hope you don't have too many shmoozing events to attend throughout the year or I guess you do since donations are important."

"Just a few each year but it's really about not having much to chat about other than my job. These people are mega rich and I am a poor surgeon who just recently paid off my student loans. So many people forget the cost of medical school and assume us doctors are living big fancy lives."

I am falling quickly. A man who is not vain and can admit he's a doctor but not rolling in money. How sweet.

Before I can reply, the waiter has returned with our bottle of Chardonnay. As he pours the wine Lucas seems nervous. He looks at the waiter and then at me.

"You know, I wanted tonight to be perfecto! I asked my godfather to prepare us a special meal and I didn't think to ask you about food allergies."

"I'm sure whatever we have will be perfect. I don't have any food allergies and there's nothing to date that I haven't tried and enjoyed."

"Ah so you have an adventurous palate!"

"I guess I do."

I smile and I see Lucas take a deep breath and sigh of relief.

Dinner was delicious and involved a fresh take on Chicken Tetrazzini as the chicken was marinated in wine for several hours. Between the Chardonnay and the chicken, I got quite the buzz for a while but thankfully we talked for hours and I am back to myself.

We walk in silence to my car and I do my best to keep my teeth from chattering as I am sure the noise would be audible to Lucas. One of the best features of my baby Range is the keyless entry. It keeps me from fumbling around in my purse for keys, which has in the past led to lengthy treasure hunts.

"Thank you for walking me to my car."

You're welcome and it's the only way to end such a beautiful night; it's the gentleman thing to do.

Ah yes! Look at that Ava! A man who knows how to be a gentleman. We are gazing into each other's eyes.

"I want to savor every minute with you. I am actually not ready to say goodnight but it is that time."

"Yes, it is."

"I would like to see you again soon. Would that be okay?"

"Most definitely."

I stare into Lucas' eyes. He's a good foot taller than me. I do love tall men. He leans over and gives me the lightest kiss on the lips and then kisses me on both cheeks. Dear god, a true gentleman.

"Goodnight Ava."

"Goodnight Lucas."

We are still staring at each other. I smile and slowly turn to open the door. As I move to get in, I notice my heart is racing. Lucas closes the door for me and I smile again as I turn on the car. I wave goodbye and drive off.

As I enter on to I-495 I let out a scream.

"Yes! This was a grownup date! Thank you, God!"

A nice quiet dinner with a smart, handsome man. No Casual Days and a DJ or people dancing around a club smoking hookahs, or a posse of friends who happened to be at the same restaurant and now let me take you home and have my way with you after our first date.

I've made it inside my apartment's garage and I am still smiling. I get out of the car and head to the elevator. As I wait for the elevator, I feel my phone vibrate. It's a text from Lucas.

Thank you for a great evening, I had a fantastic time!

The elevator doors open and I enter. I text back.

I did too! Thank you for making tonight so special!

17
Reiki Level I

It's 9 AM on a Saturday morning and I am back at the yoga studio to learn Reiki. I am excited to learn about this beautiful healing modality as I have benefited greatly from my Reiki sessions with Amy. Understanding that I can also use Reiki to help Cleo and Sophie makes this all the more intriguing as I had never thought about using the practice on animals until Amy mentioned it during our lightworker training last month.

The room is full of women and as I count, I land at 9 of us who have signed up for this class. We are sitting in a circle and Amy is explaining the history of Reiki. It is fascinating to learn how Dr. Usui could walk so beautifully in his faith take what he received as a message and turn it into this technique. This beautiful source energy flowing through us and on to others has truly transformed me.

The day is full of learning the technique and practicing on each other. I was nervous to practice but as soon as I stood over the woman I was paired with she said, "You are a healer! I can feel the heat flowing from you already!"

As I continued working on her she continued to tell me how powerful the energy was flowing through me and on to her. Eventually she fell asleep.

I thought I had done something wrong and I signaled for Amy to come over.

"Yes Ava?"

"She's asleep."

"Yes. That is something we are going to discuss shortly and I see you are getting to experience it firsthand. I knew you were a healer and this affirms it! You see, people will fall asleep sometimes when the energy is so strong."

"Are you sure she's not just tired?"

Amy laughs in a whisper.

"Granted that can happen too but we all know in this case it's you or rather is how powerful of a vessel you are!"

"Okay."

I didn't have anything more to say as I kept staring at the woman who was now snoring.

Let's let her sleep for a bit. You can finish working on her and then stand by her afterwards to ensure she is safe. We wouldn't want her to roll off the table.

"Okay, of course not."

I smiled and sighed thankful I was doing the technique correctly. I was though unsure of this power Amy and this woman say I have.

The class ended with an attunement ceremony and me driving home thinking about this powerful energy flowing through me. I am recalling being at a meeting a few months ago that Amy invited me too. It was a meeting to discuss volunteering with local homeless shelters. We ended the meeting with a heart and hand prayer where we placed our right hand on the back of the person next to us. After the prayer the woman I had my hand on looked at me in amazement. She said, "My goodness! Your hands feel like fire! What a powerful healer you are!"

I looked over at Amy who was smiling assuredly.

"Indeed, she is!"

I responded with a thank you though I wasn't sure what I was thanking them for. Now here I am today with more affirming of my gift. I never feel any heat coming from my hands but I guess that's a good thing. Probably God's way of keeping me humble.

Facebook, Dec 11, 2016

Inching closer to my first book publication so it's time to start working on the marketing plan! Thanks Shanna for the sneak peek of yesterday's shoot!

Seeing these photos of me looking like one of those authors on their book jacket cover has fired me up. I'm feeling great about my writing. I did a photoshoot so I can get my writing website to look decent. I know if I stay faithful, I will truly have all I want as Ms. Ross said. The advice I received from the agent in LA was to pick one thing and work to get it out but I'm toggling between the children's book and the novel. The advice I received at the film school in LA was to write about what I know, which is the Pentagon. So, I go to work each day unmoved about being there, come home and work on the novel and then spend a little time on my website since the children's story is already written. It's now with the illustrator and so far, the illustrations she's shared with me are breathtaking! My little babies have been turned into characters in a story! I am on track to hand it over to a local bookstore next week who will format, print and sell it. I know seeing Cleo and Sophie's book in a bookstore will amp up my novel writing even more.

I thought returning to the building would be fun, and I would have a keen eye for things to add to the novel but most days I'm a robot. At least as far as the work goes. I do though need to tune in more so I can flesh this novel out more.

Though I am not excited to be there, I can see my peacefulness is like a breath of fresh air for those I work with. They often ask me why I am so calm. Why am I not moved by any of the daily chaos. I tell them it's because I meditate and they give me a funny look. We don't really do that here at Shawshank but I have no shame in letting them know. I did stop shy of telling them I also keep a rose quartz and blue onyx (good for removing obstructions and quieting the mind) stone behind my Big Brains Fellowship certificate. They bring me so much peace it's unbelievable. Sometimes when things get a little rough, I slide my hand behind the certificate, grab the stones and place them in my jacket pocket that way as I'm speaking with someone, I can roll them around in my hand. It makes a world of difference. I've grown so much as I've learned about these healing practices and while Dr. Smith has crossed my mind, I don't feel any need to start back seeing her. I am not a fan of the term alternative healing like it's some substandard way to heal. It should be called healing. Period. Nevertheless, the practices I've learned from meditation, to breathwork to crystals to yoga and Reiki are more than supportive than any session I had with Dr. Smith.

It's been a year now since I first started my meditation practice and while overall the changes are subtle, they are indeed there. I glow and grow with a magnitude of happiness. Sure, there are times when life seems to be crapping on me but the feeling of God's love and my self-love overpowers the moment. I am upset but then it is released quickly. I can no longer hold on to bad or heavy life sucking emotions. I recall this from my lessons with Nala. She said this would begin to happen. I remember thinking that sounds like a magical place to get to and now I have arrived.

I can't say when I noticed it but when things start looking bleak the feeling doesn't seem to overtake me as much as it rolls over me like a soft whisper of thought and then poof- it's gone. Yes, in those moments I may cry or have some mini fit but honestly it only last about five minutes and then all is well again. And most importantly the emotional pain never resurfaces. Thoughts may pop up in my mind about something but no feelings of sadness are attached. It's as though they are now filed away as a lesson learned and the thought feels no different than cataloging a to do list in my head.

I have been back in the D.C. area for six months and while I remember my five minute freak out on Ventura Avenue there's not one drop of emotion attached. Returning has opened doors; with my love life, with my writing career and with a deeper learning of how I can be a healer. I am at peace. And, LA isn't going anywhere though there are those who believe the next big earthquake could convert it into an island. So, I move forward and enjoy the journey.

And on this journey are some mighty good vibes which are there all the time. Funny enough after one year people tell me I am always calm, unmoved and seemingly at peace. It's indeed how I feel but for others to notice, for others to see me the way I first saw Nala, the way I still see her; that means a lot to me. She's often said she has her moments just like others who practice meditation but yet her embodied spirit of peace outweighs the bad. At least those are my words for how the beauty of meditation works for me. I am not perfect and I never will be. I am soul incarnated in a human body therefore I will think and feel; emotions are part of the human experience but the healing power of meditation minimizes and energizes.

When I am still, I hear the answers and daily meditation restores my body and soul in such a powerful way that I move! I get things done and I know what to do. The right people, the right opportunities all align because I am open to receive and stay in a flow of love, peace and thanksgiving. All that I was incarnated to do during this lifetime will manifest because I am now in receive mode because I meditate.

Everything happens for a reason. Nala's posting a meditation introductory talk for the first time on a meetup site, me casually scrolling through my emails, seeing the invite and deciding to get off of my comfy couch that night.

And the most amazing part…this is my first-year anniversary! I am excited to see all the magnificent changes yet to come as I continue this God sent practice. I know things will only get better.

Facebook, Dec 25, 2016

Merry Christmas everyone!!! Sending tons of Christmas love from these little cuties!

I decided to stay in town this year for Christmas. The truth is I enjoy spending the holidays with the girls. Last year I was at Sarah's the year before I was trying to do an *Iyanla Fix My Life* on Dan. This year it's just me, the girls and my grandmother's soul. She was here earlier today. I sensed her when I opened the cabinet for a glass. The smell that flowed out was that of her house in Alabama. I paused for a moment and thanked her for all she's done for me and the messages she's sent through Mona. I never thought about sensing her myself until today but there she was. I'm pretty sure the me of two years of go would have freaked and ran out my apartment but today I simply said thank you.

Facebook, Dec 31, 2016

God is always right and is always on time ☺ Absolutely nothing I expected to happen this time last year for 2016 has occurred in my life ☺ but instead unexpected wonderful changes and growth have engulfed my spirit and my way of life. I'm 100% certain I have no clue what's going to happen in 2017 but I am certain it will all be part of my continued journey to evolve into my best self!

I wish you all a beautiful ending to 2016 and a glorious 2017!

Facebook, Jan 8, 2017

Dr. King,

Thank you for all you've done that has led me to have this beautiful, wonderful, eclectic set of Facebook family and friends.

You paved the way for equal rights which led to me getting a job in the Midwest where I met some of the most wonderful people in the world. Your work allows me to enter business establishments where I've met many wonderful people haphazardly who are now really good friends of mine. It opened doors wider for interracial marriages which has beautifully expanded my family.

While the struggle still continues, I thank you for all you did, all it has unfolded into. May we never forget, may we always pursue for more, for better and may we always have an open heart to love everyone always.

Speaking of struggle. I just left a voicemail for Monique. It's time to let her know I need to get this thing fixed. It's been fun but it's time to get back to Ava the hardcore left brainer with a sprinkling of right brain. Lucas is great and we're connecting on so many levels but my heart is so open. I don't want to mess up the little Ava's so I think it's time to turn this device back on. I think I need to be in left brain mode when I'm around him. I'm also surprised this device hasn't had any side effects. It's been a year and a half and it just stopped working – stuck in right brain mode. Maybe my brain is slowly deteriorating and I just can't tell. Maybe that's why I think I need it to work again because any rational person would know being open to love means being open and not turning into a robot to manage your feelings.

Monique is going to be pissed when she finds out how long ago this thing broke but she'll just have to get over it. I can't imagine having spent the year in Santa Monica with it working. I would have felt the need to switch to left brain while at work and I will say I think my research paper for the fellowship was off the chain awesome having been written in right brain mode. I spoke the truth about some of our messed-up Air Force programs and policies. I held nothing back. It read more like an op ed than a research paper but it worked as I received credit for it. It was quite liberating to slam us for our mess.

Again, I digress in thought. Lucas is amazing and everything I ever thought I'd want in a man. He's kind, smart, free spirited and funny. I am truly myself with him. I am the Jessica Simpson song, *With You.* I will admit though my mind sometimes wonders to the thought of maybe I'd be me with anyone now that I've been broken open from the great gifts of life and love I received in California. I'm sure that's it though he does make it easy to feel free around him.

But I'm starting to have panic attacks. I've developed claustrophobia and I know it has to do with this new relationship. I need to be free so I've taken out my crochet braids. It's amazing what I have with Lucas and yet as I move to embrace it more, I want to run like hell away from it. He loves me and I don't do anything. I just am. I'm just me. It's wonderful but it has to come to an end. Everything good comes to an end. He's crazy, or he's cheating on me or any moment now he's going to realize he has no interest in me. I know I prayed for this and I know this is God sent but I've never gotten anything close to what I've asked for when it comes to men so how can this be? Am I ready for this great love? I prayed, I meditated with my rose quartz on being open to giving and receiving love. So, this has to be right. God wouldn't make our meeting so unique only for this man to not be the real deal. But they all end. Every relationship to date has ended. Ended badly. Sure, there were signs and sure I ignored them but just the same they came to an end.

Where are the signs with Lucas? Why is it so hard to find them? He loves me. He drives for over an hour in traffic to see me. He looks at me as if I'm the only person in this world. This all scares the shit out of me. I need Monique and more years of meditation under my belt to feel more confident and quite possibly Dr. Smith. I've been existing for over a year in right brain mode since this damn device broke and that was all fine and well while in LA and it has made my entrance back at Shawshank far more amusing but I need to clearly think. Logic. I'm missing it. I have to do a hard shift back to left brain to do my detective work on this man. That has to be the problem. I'm not using my left brain to see how shady he must really be. Don't worry little Ava's. I've got you.

Facebook, Jan 19, 2017

Amazing night at the Kennedy Center!

It was so great to spend the evening with Tammy. She is stationed at Shawshank and we've gotten to extend our friendship from the west coast to the east coast. We did though spend more time together in California as I am now back in hermit mode.

As I begin to undress, my phone rings. It's Monique.

"Hey!"

"Girl, what's up? Long time no hear."

"I know, I got caught up out in LA and kind of dropped off the planet a little bit."

"A little bit? Girl, I thought you moved to another planet. So, you know I gotta ask, what the hell is going on with my device? You know I'm supposed to check it every so often. I thought you were going to come back this way for some visits but instead I just got those whack texts from you with videos of the ocean and shit. And, you've stopped by the salon only once since you got back with your natural hair so I don't even get to be your stylist anymore."

Even though I put crochet braids and weave back in my hair over the last few months I opted to not reach out to Monique because I knew she'd ask about this device and although I kept saying I needed to talk to her about it at the same time I was happy to procrastinate in right brain mode.

"I know but I just wanted to enjoy my year and honestly I was enjoying living in right brain mode."

"Say what? You stayed in one mode for an entire year? I've done it for a week or so but not an entire year. Even I need to switch over when I'm in entrepreneurial mode. Wow, I didn't know the thing was capable of that. Honestly, I hadn't thought that part through. So, it didn't tank out on you?"

"Actually, it broke before I left and it got stuck in right brain mode. I never bothered to tell you."

"What the fuck? Ava!"

I was out for a run and I tripped and fell. I landed right on my wrist and I felt a jolt and it switched to right brain mode. I was running in left brain because I'm anal like that; always trying to do better. Anyway, when I tried to switch back the button wouldn't click. I thought immediately to call you but just as quickly I changed my mind. I had been having a rough few weeks as I was racing to get packed for LA and it seemed like right brain would help relieve some of that pressure. I was going to call you when I got settled in but I was loving the freedom of right brain mode. I wanted the time I spent there to be open and free."

"And you're calling now because?"

"Because I need to get back to reality. I have so much shit going on and I'm feeling way too much. Don't hate me."

"I ain't hating. You let me cut open your brain and implant some makeshift device in there so how can I be upset? I'm glad you got a year in right brain mode. I hope you used it well. But for real though, seriously girl you left me hanging for over a year all you ever said was yeah, it's working. I mean I should have tested it. Not like I was going to enter it a local science fair or anything but dang to find out all this time the thing hasn't been working. And what about the spare? Let me guess, you didn't even try to use it.

"I didn't, I was afraid it would work. So can I come have you check this thing out?"

"Yes, but it will have to be in a few months. I'm in South Africa."

"What?"

"Girl yeah. I've always wanted to visit and so I decided to take some time and just do the damn thing."

"Oh, okay. I'm jealous! Well, enjoy your trip!"

"Plan to. This is just the first part, from here I'm heading to Australia."

"Damn!"

"Yep, doing the damn thing! Then a hair show in New York."

"Okay well, I'll catch up with you when you get back."

"Okay. And girl I know you. Don't freak out and do anything crazy while I'm gone. You been in right brain mode for almost two years so a couple more months ain't going to do shit. Well let's hope anyway. And don't try the spare now. After all this time I can't imagine what a switch to left brain would do."

"Yeah, right. Okay. Enjoy and talk to you later."

"Peace!"

Shit! How in the hell am I supposed to continue this relationship like this?

Facebook, Feb 13, 2017

How can I start off this workweek the best way possible?...by not being at work!

Let's recap... 2015, spent my birthday in surgery. 2016 at Redondo Beach, 2017 did nothing even though I am in a relationship but at Pancake Haven in Springfield Virginia two days later but, I have the week off so let's count this blessing. And I am done with Facebook, again. This posting my life is not for me. I will focus on writing my life from now on in my semi-autobiographical novel.

I was hoping for something special with Lucas but his work schedule didn't allow for anything this week as he has surgeries scheduled every day and needs to rest during the evenings. He was so incredibly thoughtful and had five dozen red roses delivered to my apartment with a card that said we will have a belated celebration next week.

Honestly after Dan, Hookah Man and Mr. Come Home with Me, a rain check from Lucas who has been such a breath of fresh air is a giant leap forward! I will happily sit solo in this restaurant eating my pancakes because I know that next week will bring an amazing experience with him. Though I still get claustrophobic especially at night. It's like I am dying to be free hence the need to take out the crochet braids and breathe. When he spends the night, I am overjoyed until he holds me in his arms. I should be melting in this man's embrace and instead it makes the claustrophobia much worse.

Dan used to say he felt claustrophobic at times and I thought it was because of his fear of commitment but how can that be the case for me when this is what I've been waiting on for so long? Fear, I guess. Fear this isn't real, won't last or both. Being in right brain mode all happy with no way to logically process this is killing me. Though I think if I were to check in with Dr. Smith, she would tell me I should be feeling it and not trying to rationalize the hell out of it.

I know I've got much more work to do before I can relax into a good healthy relationship and I also know my time with Lucas may be short because of it. I can see myself running him away. Not for any reason but that I just don't know how to swim in the deep end if you know what I mean. I can tell he is trying to have patience with me when I overly thank him for doing something that is just normal kindness like calling to say hello. I think he's beginning to feel sorry for me and less attracted to me as I am not showing myself to be the self-confident woman he thought he met.

We'll see. I am not going to die if Lucas fades out of my life but damn, he really is everything I'd hoped for with the exception of his ethnicity. I thought I'd find this kind of love with a black man and I still have a longing to be with a good brother. Someone who can relate to my struggles as a black person. Lucas grew up in Argentina and came here for medical school. He says he gets it as a person of color but he really doesn't, at least not a person of color from this country.

I felt solidarity with Dan. It was nice to talk about the blatant discrimination from white folks and even though he's from Chicago he understands chitlins and ham hocks as part of Christmas dinner and just black life in general. But I don't want to be ungrateful either. I just feel Lucas may be here to further help me in getting my shit together as it relates to romantic relationships. As much as I want to go from baby steps to running a marathon all with the same man, I can see where this is probably not going to be the case.

I am now remembering alternate nostril breathing! How could I forget as I recently learned this practice. I take a seat in my meditation space in my bedroom and Cleo and Sophie happily curl up next to me. I start by inhaling and exhaling in each nostril then I move to only inhaling an exhaling from my right nostril. I do several rounds and stop. I then do the same with my left nostril. I take note of the feelings from each approach and then go back to inhaling and exhaling through my right nostril. I can feel the difference. It's not as strong as the device but there is a pull on my left brain and I feel that logic, rational vibe kick in.

Hell yeah! Okay Monique, enjoy your trips. I got this and I am doing it with breathwork! Now how to dissect this Lucas thing? I look around for my journal, grab it and begin to write.

Ava, you are falling in love with a wonderful man. You are still healing from your childhood trauma and you need to be gentle with yourself. You healed a lot with your hypnotherapy with Amy last year and now that you are dating someone you are experiencing triggers. You are okay and you are safe to explore your feelings. Perhaps Lucas is not forever and that's fine. Just allow yourself to continue to heal and enjoy the journey!

I read my words a few times and smile. Yeah, I'm going to be just fine.

18
Published Author

I am bubbling with excitement as I wait for Mary. Today is the day I pick up my books! As I wait, I see my book, *The Adventures of Cleo and Sophie - Trip to the Moon* on display as a new release. This is real and yet feels surreal at the same time. I have become a published author thanks to the bookstore's self-publishing services.

I am recalling the encouragement I received a couple of years ago from a literary agent. She loved the concept and said it had potential to be adapted into a cartoon series. I remember the thrill I felt from this news and the immediate lackluster feeling that followed. Back then, just two years ago I had no confidence in myself. I had no belief that anything that great would happen for me and so even with this highly encouraging news I found myself procrastinating and diving deep into the groundhog work of Shawshank. Thank you, God, for my time in California and the awakening of my soul and self-esteem!

"Ava!"

"Hi Mary!"

"Are you excited?"

"So excited! Thank you for everything! The book is wonderful and the way you laid out the story with the illustrations is perfect."

"You're welcome! Your book is too cute! I am sure you are going to sell many copies."

Mary walks behind her desk and pulls out a box.

"Here are your 50 copies to sell as you wish. Were you able to upload it on online?"

"Yes, it's available to purchase on multiple sites and I really can't thank you enough."

"It was my pleasure. You said you are also working on a novel?"

"Yes, I am almost done so I will be reaching out soon for your support with it as well."

"Sounds great and don't forget to stop by the children's section and see your book on display there as well."

"I certainly will."

I take the box of books and head downstairs. I walk into the children's section and there it is! My book on a display stand with several copies flanked around it.

"May I help you find something," asks the sales lady".

"Oh no I just wanted to see my book on display and take a picture if that's okay."

"You are the author of Cleo and Sophie?"

"Yes, I am."

"Oh, this is such a delightful book! We've already sold 10 copies and we just added it to the inventory a few days ago."

"Really?"

"Um hum. The children love the dogs, and the activity pages at the back of the book."

"That is so wonderful to hear, thank you!"

The saleslady smiles and begins to walk off as I take a few pictures of the display.

"Hey, why don't I take one of you?"

"Thanks!"

I hand her my phone and stand next to my books smiling.

"Here you go!"

"I appreciate you so much!"

"You're quite welcome."

I pick up the box and head out to my car. Once inside I open the box, peep inside and smile. I did this and this is just the beginning. I can feel my energy rising and the smile broadening on my face. I have come so far in a short time and I am so grateful for every part of my journey.

19

Back at Shawshank

My life has good days and days when I skipped my morning meditation and I should've at least stuck a sodalite crystal in my pocket before heading out of the door. Friday was one of those days. Today I returned to work after taking a week off for my birthday. I know having the crystal in my pocket for the short 15 minute walk to Shawshank would have made it better. I wasn't remotely rested having spent my entire time off working to resurrect my dog walking business and running a host of other errands. So, it should not have been a surprise when I knocked over my latte and it spilled all over the office floor. To make up for it I returned downstairs, purchased a larger latte, and made peace with the situation.

To avoid the attraction of the many rodents I am sure reside in the building, I called the custodial service for a spot clean.

The buzzer sounds and I head to the door. I open the door and standing in front of me is a short Hispanic man with a carpet shampoo machine. He is grinning from ear to ear.

"Hello, thanks for coming."

He nods and follows me into the office.

As I walk him to my desk, he looks around the office smiling.

"You like it here, yes?"

"No, actually I don't."

"Sure, you do! You get to do fun stuff!"

I am not sure what he thinks we do here but fun is not a word I would use for my groundhog days at Shawshank.

He searches for an outlet and begins steam cleaning the coffee saturated spot by my chair. As he does, Ted returns from his meeting and joins me by the copier.

"I can't believe you have this nice man cleaning. Look around at all the other stains we have."

"I know but I don't want to be the one who brings the rats."

"The rats are already here. I've seen them. You have too, you just don't want to admit it."

"Okay, sure outside. I was leaving a little after midnight during closeout (end of the fiscal year, September 30th a.k.a Hell Night) and saw a bunch of them running around a construction zone but I'd like to think they stay outside."

"Sure, they do."

I expected this to take a few minutes but to my surprise he keeps going, he cleans my entire area and then moves on to Ted's area and then on to the entire office. People look confused but also thankful and happily move out of his way.

It's been about thirty minutes and his dedication to doing a good job – going above and beyond what was expected of him is striking to me. Here he is exerting extra energy to give us a clean work area and I was struggling just prior to his arrival with mustering up enough concern to write five sentences for my boss.

I used to go above and beyond and now I'm so underwhelmed I can't get up enough brain power to write five sentences. This man gets paid a fraction of what I make and he has more love and dedication than I think I will ever have again for this place.

After a week off all I thought about this morning when I woke up was I am thankful for another day of life and I am now more motivated than ever to get the hell out of Shawshank! It must be done. I don't love anything I do here, don't like it, can't tolerate it, can't lie to myself about it anymore. I bet he woke up thankful for another day of life and thankful for his job. Perhaps he really loves what he does. Maybe this is all he does, carpet cleaning. Maybe he drowns out the crazy with that loud vacuum and is in his world all day. I bet he can be in the present moment a lot more than I am able to be. Although I do try, I find I am forever escaping my work and the specific task at hand, the opposite of what Eckhart Tolle recommends. Instead, I am daydreaming of freedom.

I think God made today extremely uncomfortable for me and that is how the latte spilled. It was so I could remember that I really am not supposed to be here but for a moment like a journalist getting all my data to finish this novel about this bureaucratic foolishness and it becomes a number one bestseller. I will discuss my inspirational fiction with Oprah on Super Soul Sunday and Quentin Tarantino and Shonda Rhimes will work with me to make it a movie, a blockbuster hit which will then turn into the number one all-time rated television series that will be picked up around the world! And Cleo and Sophie's book will be the most popular cartoon show ever! My work will educate, inspire and entertain. I will be living in my purpose and doing my part to uplift the masses! Yep, I've got big dreams and they ain't got shit to do with Shawshank – well other than using it to write my way to freedom.

I have fully drifted off into my fantasy when the nice man walks up to me with his vacuum smiling.

"Thank you so much! You made our office clean again!"

"My pleasure ma'am! I love to get things bright and shiny."

I knew it! This man really loves what he does! I only love writing and not five unnecessary sentences for my boss to recite to his SES like he came up with the brilliance that lies within those five sentences. Yeah, I hate this place but I can do any of these jobs with my eyes closed though I guess many of us can because that's how bureaucracy works.

20
Mammograms Suck

I'm sitting in the waiting room or shall I say the third waiting room as I await the third set of tests from my mammogram. I have very dense fibrocystic breasts. This was first discovered when I was 13 years old and a lump started growing in my left breast. I remember every detail of the day I had the lump removed. It was at a hospital in New Jersey and the doctor spent the entire time talking to the nurse about how European doctors were far more educated than American doctors. I was 13 and I knew this didn't sound good since he was American. When he was done and oh by the way he didn't put me to sleep he just numbed my breast and told me to turn my head and not look. So, when this whole thing was over, he asked the nurse if they had any of the thread that doesn't leave a scar. She said not nearby but on another floor. He was not interested in waiting for her to get it and as a result I have a big scar on my breast. I now have three more scars from other biopsies.

But I digress. I'm freezing. I hate these tiny hospital semi gown things you wear for mammograms and why in the world do they make you wait so long?

"Ms. McClure? A doctor walks into the one person waiting room and closes the door."

"We see a little something and we would like to do a biopsy."

"Oh?"

"Yes, it's not particularly concerning but we would like to know for sure as you are getting older."

My look of confusion must be making her uncomfortable.

"I just mean I know you've been getting these masses in your breasts since you were 13 and well now that you're in your mid 40s we have to just be mindful of all possibilities."

"Right. Sure. Yes of course. I understand what you're saying."

"Great. We can go down the hall and you can schedule the biopsy. It'll just be a very small incision and we will have the results in a few days."

"Sure," I say.

She opens the door, walks me down the hall and motions for me to walk in a room. I see a young doctor sitting at a computer with images of my breasts. She magnifies an area and points at the screen.

"This is our concern. You see how the right side of the mass takes on an odd shape? That's what makes this not like the cysts you've had removed."

I smile and nod my head.

The first doctor smiles and points across the hall.

"They will schedule your biopsy."

"Okay," I say and slowly glide across the hall.

Did I have questions? Of course I had questions. But none were coming out of my mouth just now. Being in my mid 40s the doctor is right. It isn't to be assumed it's the same thing that I've had since I was 13. I'm starting to feel a sense of panic and worry and I'm beginning to feel nauseous. I am just coming into my place of peace and happiness and I don't need this news to shake that. I take a few deep breaths and smile as I walk across the hall to schedule my appointment. As I exit the room and head down the hallway to the elevators, I think to myself I know I'm here for something big so this is nothing. I declare it so because I don't have time for it. I am in the best place in my life and I am in perfect health.

Now that's how you live a positive thinking life! I am seeing the changes in me from the many practices I learned in California, my sessions with Amy and from her lightworker and Reiki I classes. My life is ten times better all because I take time for me each day.

21
Date Night

I made it through the week and it's Friday evening. I am dressed in a black silk sleeveless dress, ruby red stilettos, and big silver hoop earrings. The girls are curled up on the couch watching me pace back and forth as I wait for Lucas. He was supposed to be here an hour ago and I have not heard from him. I'm sure he's caught up at the hospital but it doesn't stop me from worrying. He's always called or texted if he was running even a few minutes late but again I am sure he's probably still in surgery. Plus, I am sure some of my anxiety stems from my mammogram exam this afternoon.

I walk into the bathroom to pat my face. I have yet to discover a makeup brand that can keep me from shining for more than an hour. As I touch up my face my phone rings and startles me. I'm not sure why since I'm expecting to hear from Lucas but just the same my heart starts racing and as I turn to exit the bathroom I almost trip. I pick up the phone which is lying on the kitchen island and see that it is Lucas. I answer.

"Hey!"

"Ava, I am so incredibly sorry. I had an emergency surgery this afternoon and ran into several complications. I am just finishing up but I can be at your place in an hour."

"That is so thoughtful of you to still want to meet up but I completely understand if you would rather go home and rest for the evening."

"What I want is to spend the evening and night with you that is if you'll have me."

"Of course, but how about instead of a night out we spend the night in?"

"I'm really okay to go out. I'm a big boy and I know my limits. Besides, I've got a few special things planned for you and even though we are a little behind schedule everything can be adjusted. You my beautiful lady can have your celebration tonight."

"I won't argue with that and I'm looking forward to what the night has in store. I'll see you soon."

"I'll be there as quickly as I can."

I hang up the phone wanting to kick myself in the ass. I did it again. I'm always over accommodating always wanting to dim my light and I can see that this frustrates him. Why can't I be okay with someone wanting to do something wonderful for me? Because no one ever has. I have been doing my alternate nostril breathing and focusing on my left brain and the answer is clear. Now comes more work to embrace my worthiness. I know it will happen; I just have to be gentle with my healing process.

Forty-five minutes later there is a knock at my door. The girls jump off the couch and walk with me. I open the door and I am greeted with a sheepish grin from Lucas who is handsomely cloaked in a black wool coat and burgundy scarf around the collar. His hands are behind his back as he walks in and kisses me on the lips. Normally he would play with the girls but he is determined to keep whatever is behind his back a mystery. Cleo and Sophie continue to dance on their hind legs with excitement for his presence.

"Hey babies! Give me one minute and I will give you some love!"

I close the door and when I turn around Lucas is on his knees with a box in his hand.

We just met two months ago so I am one hundred percent convinced there's no ring in this box but I am curious as to what's inside.

"Ava, we've known each other for a while now."

I smile. Okay maybe I am wrong and there is a ring in there? Maybe two months is a while and there are people who've gotten engaged after a couple of months or even weeks of dating. My heart is now racing. Before I can respond, Lucas opens the box and reveals a shiny gold key. Oh, thank god.

Would you do me the honor of moving in with me?

While I am thankful it's a key and not a ring, I am still speechless.

"Lucas. Wow I…"

"I know we've only known each other two months but these two months have been better than any I've ever had with anyone else."

And here I am thinking my insecurities are running him away.

"Yes!"

What did I just say?

"I knew it! I knew we were on the same page!"

Lucas takes the key out of the box and hands it to me. I take it and begin to rub it like it's one of my crystals.

"Ava, I want to take care of you. I want you to be able to live a wonderful life, write your novel and not worry about anything. I'll take care of everything. You don't have to worry about money or bills and you can quit your job and write fulltime."

I know I should be ecstatic but I can't get there. I've got so much self-work to do. How can Lucas not see this? We've talked about our previous relationships and while he's saying that I'm the best he's ever had and Lord knows he's the best I've ever had, does that make it the best we'll ever have? Maybe that's the wrong question. The question is even if we are the best we'll ever have should we jump the living together broom so quickly? We don't even have keys to each other's homes but now I have an invitation to move in with him. And Lucas is not rolling in money as he just paid off his student loans so how would this work?

In the middle of this fairy tale moment, I am contemplating how I could have something better but it's not better in the sense that it's better than Lucas it's better in the sense that I know I have so much more I need to discover about myself. My word I just took all of my crochet braids out and did the big chop with my hair because I was feeling claustrophobic because this man makes me feel too great. Now I'm happy but sad because this wonderful Latino man isn't black but he's here on bended knee handing me a key and wanting me to move in with him. Honest to goodness I think I might be experiencing a twilight zone moment.

"You're quiet. I know this was not what you were expecting as a belated birthday present."

"I wasn't but it's wonderful!"

I try to sound shocked and excited.

We love each other and this is the best relationship either of us have experienced. We are in our forties and we know what's out there, we know what we want and we have that with each other.

Do we though? Maybe this is the best of everything. I mean no one's perfect, everyone's always got some other layer of healing to do. What exactly am I looking for – for me to be perfect before a man would want to spend the rest of his life with me? That's absurd and Dr. Smith would say exactly those words. I am sure this is what healing looks like; knowing that you are better than you were while still working on your shit. You have someone great in your life who can see the effort you're putting into becoming a stronger person and they love you.

What's interesting is I don't have anything to compare this to. I have no sense of what love feels like not even platonic and certainly not from my family. I've never experienced it before so how in the hell am I supposed to know that this is actually it?

I look at Lucas who is smiling as I am smiling so he is none the wiser that all these thoughts are racing through my head. He stands up and we kiss passionately. Cleo and Sophie dance around on their hind legs full of joy. I look to them for their approval as dogs know better than humans about the character of a person and they love Lucas so I know he's a good man.

Lucas bends down and places the box on the coffee table. He then gives tons of love to Cleo and Sophie. I stare at the key in my hand as he plays with them.

"Ready for dinner?"

"Yes, where are we going?"

"Now you know that's a surprise."

"Okay."

I smile brightly at Lucas as he reaches for my coat on the couch. He helps me put it on and says, "By the way you look hot! I love your hair this way!"

"Thank you, sweetie!"

I kiss him gently on the lips and wrap my arms around him. He gives me a tight hug.

"Okay babies! We'll see you later!"

Even the way he speaks to the girls is so incredible. I love that he's a dog person and I love him so much.

"Bye babies", I say as we head out.

Crystal City becomes a ghost town around 5 PM on Fridays and doesn't awake until Monday mornings so we have the entire sidewalk to ourselves as we make our way to Lucas' car.

"You know I was worried you would say no."

"Really?"

I thought you'd say it was too soon but I couldn't hold back any longer. I want to see you every day. I want to play with Cleo and Sophie every night when I get home from work. I want to sleep next to you and wake up knowing you are next to me.

Damn I hit the mother lode.

Lucas opens the passenger door and I get in. He joins me in the car, leans over and kisses me on the cheek.

"I want those things too. I've never felt so strongly for anyone before."

"Me either."

We begin to kiss. Our kissing turns into touching and I find Lucas' hand sliding up my dress and my hand gripping his crotch. I want him to take me right here on 15th Street. His fingers are now rubbing on my panties and he is moving my panties to the side and sliding his finger inside me. As he fucks me with his finger I moan in delight. I move to unzip his pants and expose his long hard erection. I am now climaxing and I feel my body release wetness that shows as Lucas removes his finger. It's now my turn to delight him and I do so by taking all of his length into my mouth. His enjoyment is audible with heavy panting and moaning. He reluctantly pulls away. I sit up and smile. I know he wants to delay his climax for later and him almost reaching it now is going to make for an amazing night.

"Baby! You know it's going to be hard for me to get through dinner now?"

"Why is that", I ask with a smirk.

"Because I now want to make love to you so bad."

"I want us to make love all night."

"Oh, we will don't you worry."

I zip his pants up and straighten up my dress. He starts the car and we drive off. So, let's recap. You have a hot Latino man who loves you, wants you to move in with him, loves your dogs and always delivers mad passionate love making like no one you've ever dated. Problem? Many actually but for tonight I am going to do my present moment thing.

I wake up still spinning from last night. After dinner Lucas and I came back to his place and we made love all night. Our passion was intense. I've never felt my body melt into a man but last night we were one and the heat that rose in our bodies glistened as beads of sweat rolling down our hot naked bodies. Reliving the moment is making my body quiver and I squirm with delight.

I look at the nightstand and see I have a text from the pet sitter. The only hint I got about my birthday celebration was to book the sitter.

I turn to see Lucas asleep facing me. I take a moment to study him. The firmness of his cheekbones, his golden wavy hair, how his eyelashes move up and down ever so slightly as he breathes.

I didn't tell him about the biopsy. I thought about it but decided to keep my positive thoughts and not share this news. If I talk about it will bring up the worry that I have squashed so it's best to say nothing at least for now. I know if I need him, he will be there for me.

We are together, a couple. We are moving in together. We are passionate for each other and every part of our lives together is amazing. I think though we are still in the honeymoon stage. What do they say? How long before people show their true colors? It could be just the sex. What if this is just the next part of my healing phase? What if this is a way to release energy, a way to let go, be free? Even if I have to stay at Shawshank a little bit longer there's freedom in letting go and being my true sexual self. Lucas is my vessel for healing or at least one of them as there is also Mona and Amy and I release greatly during deep tissue massages so yeah, that's what he is.

Do I know this to be true? Not at all. I love him. Even spending time in left brain mode with my breathwork I know this. The only illogical thing is moving in together two months after meeting but what's the worst that can happen? It doesn't work out? I don't plan to quit my job and write fulltime so I know there's part of me that is using my left brain in this situation. Plus, if I quit, I would owe the government about fifty thousand dollars to payback the fellowship and there is no way in hell I am going to pay them to leave.

I close my eyes and rest in the quiet. As I begin to drift off to sleep, I feel a gentle kiss on my lips.

"I love you, Ava."

I open my eyes to Lucas' piercing blue eyes and smile.

"I love you, Lucas."

I slide closer to him and he pulls me closer into a tight hug. He kisses me on the forehead and we drift off to sleep.

22

Bringing Shawshank Home

For the first time in my one year and some months of meditating I woke up this morning still thinking about the events of work from Friday with thoughts of how I would tell these people off on Monday. I will never understand how we, the Air Force, can't just stay in our lane.

We received a question from The Hill asking if we needed additional dollars for our fighter fleet. The answer seemed simple to me. Nope, but of course that was not the case.

Lt Col Insecure was insistent we provide rationale for more funding to which I said, "But our numbers are correct. What if we respond with our budget is correct, we know what we are doing thanks for asking."

"You're kidding right?"

"No, I'm not Mike. The Hill is asking because they assume we made a mistake in our budget calculations. We look good responding with we know how to formulate our budget requirements. To go back and say oops we made a mistake like our sister service just makes us look incompetent."

"We can't let additional funding just slip away from us. Do you know how many other programs would jump on this and say yes?"

"It's not a competition."

"Yes, it is."

"No, it's taxpayers' dollars and we should be responsible, you know, good stewards of the taxpayers' dollars. I prefer not to go back asking for something we don't need."

"That's not going to happen so I suggest you get your team to pull together a response with some new budget figures we can send up to the Chief to approve."

"What I'm going to do is take my team and head to Baskin Robbins. They're drained from all the unnecessary taskers this week and they need a break. If you would like to respond to senator Drake by all means you can craft a response and push it forward but I will not."

"But this is your area of expertise. You manage this portion of the budget."

"Exactly and I know we don't need any more money. For me to say this indicates I didn't do my job correctly. Have you even thought about that?"

"What I know is no one in our leadership is going to let us get away with a we're good thank you response."

"Sadly, you are correct but I'm refusing to do it so do what you like."

Mike looked furious and confused as he walked away from my desk. I didn't care and I still feel like there's more I need to say on Monday about all of this. We work ourselves into some type of frenzy over absolutely nothing every day. There's a drudge and toll to keep hammering out responses to questions from The Hill and questions from our leadership all the while our budgets rarely change and this place could literally operate with probably two people yet here we are, all 26,000 of us working unnecessary taskers in a continuous do-loop of foolery.

The day ended wonderfully as my team enjoyed the break and the team building time. I am blessed to have them. They are a unique collection of personalities from young to middle age from military to civilian. They work hard and are dedicated to doing their best and some days it makes me a smidge bit motivated to engage more but for the most part I am the advisor, spiritual counselor and wellness coach. On any given day you can walk past their four quad cubicle and see me sitting in the middle of them doing breathwork. Many think we're nuts but it's what keeps us sane. This week was extra stressful with a ton of taskers and while we did breathwork and got in a few meditations we needed a change of scenery. The thirty minutes out of the office served as a recharge to get through the last few hours of the week.

All in one day I went from Shawshank crazy to mammograms and biopsies to a wonderful belated birthday celebration with Lucas and I feel as though I need to balance my Chakras as they all feel out of alignment. I pick up my Chakra book and begin searching for an exercise that will support balancing them. I decide on crystal healing and I am now lying on the living room floor in Shavasana with crystals on my body. My eyes are closed and Cleo and Sophie are curled up on either side of me. This feels good. I'm grounded and aligned.

23

Massage Table Claustrophobia

I am feeling better as I used the crystal healing exercise from my Chakra book. Today I am treating myself to a ninety-minute-deep tissue massage. Massages are a great way to release tension and toxins in the body and I know this will also help me to fully reset.

I am naked under the sheets with my face snug in the face cradle. The pressure the massage therapist is using is a hurts so good kind of pressure and I am overjoyed as I feel the tension leave my body. He leans in and applies a magnificently painful pressure to my shoulders and as he works out the tension my heart begins to race. I feel a deep sense of panic with my face burrowed in this face cradle and I am doing all I can to not jump up and hop off. I'm not sure what's happening as I enjoy massages and I am very used to the face cradle but for some reason I can't keep my face in here. I feel as if I'm about to explode. There is an overwhelming sense of nervous energy pulsating throughout my body and my heart feels like a ticking timebomb.

I don't even know if this is considered claustrophobia since my eyes are not covered and I can see the floor well as best I can anyway since it's dark in the room. I know I'm perfectly safe but I feel as though a dark heavy cloak has come over me and is suffocating me.

Okay Ava, take some deep breaths and calm down you're being absolutely ridiculous right now. Why in the world am I having a claustrophobic moment on a massage table? I should be enjoying this.

I am enjoying this, aren't I? I'm beginning to sense that this has something to do with Lucas and it has something to do with me feeling trapped in this amazing relationship with this man. I thought I had worked through this with my alternate nostril breathing and focusing on my left brain but this feels like it did before I took out my crochet braids.

This doesn't make any sense to me. I am meditating. I'm using my crystals. I'm doing breathwork and I go to yoga classes. I'm doing everything right so what the freak frack is wrong with me? Lucas and I are great, we are moving in together and sure that's a change that doesn't include returning to LA but not panic attack worthy. I'm beginning to understand it's never been about Lucas. It's never been about embracing this amazing man and this incredible relationship. My suffocating crochet braid experience and now this claustrophobic face cradle nightmare has nothing to do with him at all. Well, I can't say that. It definitely has something to do with the fact that my life is changing but it's not just the releasing of my fear of commitment or fear of being with a wonderful man. It's the overall idea of moving and changing. The panic is fear of change. Changing into an entirely new mindset. Change that has insecurities identified and doing the work to heal and a completely new world of love and light for myself. Lucas is only a symptom. The root cause is this new Ava is more self-assured, stronger, open to magic and mysticism. She is light and lifted and that old me is trying to hang on for dear life.

I wonder if slaves felt this way out there picking cotton or tobacco or whatever they were doing in the house or possibly getting raped somewhere on the plantation. Whatever they were doing did they have panic attacks thinking about running away and having a better life? I'm sure they did and they had good reason to but here I am free as a bird and freaking out over having the life I desire. Makes sense though as they say if you're not uncomfortable you're not growing. I can appreciate being uncomfortable but disruption of my deep tissue massage is unacceptable.

I feel a smile on my face as I let out a deep sigh and feel my body relax again. Little Avas, we are worthy and deserving of all the good things we are experiencing. No need to panic. I am going to keep us safe.

24
Life with Lucas

I love my life with Lucas. I smile as I make dinner and watch Lucas play with Cleo and Sophie. It occurred to me that I haven't told Lucas about the biopsy because I'm used to keeping everything to myself. That's what I do. I never ask for help. That's how I ended up taking a bus to a surgery two years ago and taking a car service home. I never like to ask people to help me with anything. I never want to be a burden. I know this stems from my childhood as I always felt I was a burden to my parents. I need to work to heal this to continue to keep my little Avas safe. Lucas would want to know and he would offer such great support, for goodness sakes the man's a doctor. I'm sure he could offer some advice, comfort or something even though breasts aren't his specialty, least not medically though he does know how to work his tongue around my nipples.

I place the vegan casserole in the oven, set the timer and take a deep breath. I join Lucas on the floor with Cleo and Sophie.

"Dinner will be ready in thirty minutes."

"I can't wait to try your vegan dish. You delight me with your bacon cheeseburgers one day and vegan cooking the next."

"I believe we should eat what we want, in moderation of course."

I smile and give Lucas a kiss.

"I agree with you, of course I am far less healthy in my food choices than you."

I laugh as I throw a toy to Sophie and give Cleo a belly rub. Lucas wraps his arms around me and pulls me close for a tight hug.

"So, when are you guys moving in?"

I take a look around at my place.

"Well, I don't have much so we can do that soon."

"Are you still okay with it?"

"Yes, I am excited though I am going to have to get used to living in the District. I'm spoiled with my fifteen-minute walk to work each day but being with you is worth the commute."

"Or, I can move to Crystal City. We can get a bigger place here and I can rent my house."

"Oh no! The girls love your backyard and I love your hot tub", I laugh.

"Yeah, I love spending time with you in our hot tub."

"Yes, our hot tub."

Lucas kisses me gently on my forehead. I feel grounded and safe but not because of Lucas because I am finally standing in my self-worth.

"I had a mammogram last week and they want me to have a biopsy."

"Really?"

Lucas' face has gone from love and happiness to concern.

"Yes, but I've had a few over the years as you know and they said it's most likely nothing but because of my age and the shape of the mass they want to be certain."

"Sure, yes that is the best approach. When is the biopsy?"

"In two weeks."

"Okay, I'll be there for you."

Lucus says this with certainty and almost like an order.

"I know you've had a few of these in the past and you have a few sexy reminders on your breasts so I get it may not be a big deal but just the same let me support you, please."

"I am grateful you want to. I'll text you the date and time."

"That casserole is smelling delicious!"

"Let's hope it tastes as good as it smells. This is my first time trying the recipe."

"If not, we can make it a bacon cheeseburger night."

We laugh and kiss.

Thank you, God, for my blessed life.

Lucas. Sexy hot Lucas. I love this wonderful man and he sends me text message like:

My beautiful, sweet Ava! I have waited my entire life for you. You are the woman God created for me. My love for you overflows into every cell in my body. I bathe in your essence when I think of you.

I want to give all of myself to you. I want to fill you with my body and delight you as you deserve.

And a typical text from me:

My love, I know it's possible to love you even more than I do and today proves to be an occurrence of my love expanding for you. All day I have been feeling this overwhelming sense of love for you as if my heart is expanding every second and as it does it aches and yearns for you. I long to be in your embrace. I am flooded with joy for you. Thinking of you makes my heart pound harder with every passing second.

I want to express my love for you beyond words. I want to kiss you beyond any passion imaginable. I want you to feel my love for you deep inside me. I want our bodies to intertwine and become one moving in a rhythm that only our souls can understand. I want to give all of myself to you all of the time.

When I thought I would get one of the jobs I applied for in LA I decided to reopen my perfectfit.com and alignment.com accounts. I even got crazy and reactivated my blackfolksconnect.com account. I love my black brothers but that site has some interesting characters on it. I was excited to meet the men of LA County and while I prefer the old fashion conventional way, I had to accept that dating sites were indeed the new way of meeting someone.

I wasn't ready though. I just wanted Dan to want me. But as I think back on most of my relationships that's all I've wanted from any of them. For them to want me for me, to be someone they found worthy of being with. Clearly this came from lack of feeling loved as a child but even knowing this, even with the hypnotherapy session with Amy, even with the newfound joy from meditation I still struggle on occasion with self-love. I understand it's a process and in time I will get there.

I see clearly now that's my issue with Lucas. I still don't love me enough to know he loves me for me. He is doing what I wanted the others to do and he does want me. We connect better than anyone I've dated in the past but it's me who is not yet connected with me as deeply as I can be. This is no different than that vanilla latte. Nope Oprah, still not ready for the chai tea latte. I have though started watching Telemundo in hopes of learning Spanish again so I can communicate with Lucas in his native language even though I know he will not be in my life much longer. I know this because I need to step back and do some deeper work on me.

25
This Place

Today I made it up to the third floor on the escalator before I remembered I fucking hate this place. I hate the slave-like mentality of this place. I hate the institution, the fake Stepford Wives smiles, the Groundhog Days. I am beginning to see that meditation is opening me up to see the truth of this place. Sure, I've always called it Shawshank and joked about it being the remake of *Groundhog Day* but now I really see and feel it. There is a hollowness in this place that can never be filled and not to mention we work in a place that fell victim to 9/11. This place is a spiritual gravesite. People died in this building and their memorial is here on the Reservation as we call it.

This thought haunts me. How many times have I been on that side of the building? Too many. For years I've passed by without much thought. They removed the remains of those who died, rebuilt the corridor and people went back to work. This goes beyond Groundhog Day and Shawshank and into the movie *The Others*.

Those people died from a planned attack. I work for an agency that plans for war. We strategize, play war games, and execute with a ferocious vengeance. The building is the giver of many attacks and those attacks resulted in thousands of deaths - both the enemy and our own. The building is also the receiver of a vicious attack. The bloodstains cloak this place yet we walk around as though they don't exist except for the visual evidence of the soldiers – the heroes, the ones who deployed far too many times during the last two wars in the

Middle East. No doubt we feel their energy which harbors war, death and destruction, separation from family, friends and loved ones. How can this place be anything but darkness? How could we possibly muster up anything more than our Stepford Wives smiles?

Perhaps a monk or some spiritual guru could work here and be unaffected but I am a newbie to all these practices. I feel like there aren't enough meditations, breathwork, yoga classes and Reiki sessions to ever fully be unaffected by this place. Hence the eagle Amy saw pecking at my head during my session.

My favorite dining option, my sacred basement restaurant, is closed until further notice. Seeing that sign the other day when all I wanted was a bacon cheeseburger and fries helped me understand that maybe I should be closed until further notice as well. Meaning as much as others are in awe of my transformation to a calm person, I am an empath and now that I know this, I am more motivated to free myself after this last sentence I signed up for. Every few months I calculate how much I still owe for taking the fellowship. I am just approaching one year back so four years or forty-eight thousand dollars.

26

Black Folks at Shawshank

There are two things I always do in meetings. The first is look at pictures in the conference room. While I've been in many, I still intentionally look to see there are no black leaders on the wall because we have not had any at the highest ranks – the wall worthy ranks that is.

The second thing I do after all these years is take a quick count to see how many black people are in the meetings I attend. Usually, it's one or two but the other week I was in a meeting with all black people. It was good, successful. It was in sync and I don't think we'll have anything like it again. I shouldn't say this as hopefully we have more productive meetings but I guess I'm just being cynical. You set a pretty high bar when you have high productivity levels here at Shawshank and to think this meeting happened with all black people probably shocks the shit out of many people or perhaps it doesn't, I mean after all we were the workers on the plantations. It was us getting things done - always has been, always will be.

And there are those white folks that always fascinate me in meetings. That person who is neither a General nor a SES but insist that they are important enough to sit at the table with the big boys and girls and then fall asleep. I wonder why that doesn't bother these people? I wonder if there's some lack of concern or do they not know they're falling asleep? Surely, they know and why are they not extremely embarrassed? And why in the world do you insist on sitting at the table knowing you're going to fall asleep? Puzzling but I did once attend a meeting with a 2- Star who afterwards said he got in a good nap so maybe not as puzzling as I think and not just limited to the worker bees who dare sit at the table.

Today I'm in one of those meetings. I am watching Jasper -not his real name, it's his call sign nodding off at the table. We are sitting here discussing what should be important, the upcoming FYDP (future years defense program) for the flying hour program and Jasper who is a retired Lieutenant Colonel now a GS-15 is sitting at the table with a bunch of two stars. I'm briefing several programming options and he is nodding off so hard I can't believe the heavy dropping of his head doesn't wake him up. I want to stop my briefing and throw something at him. I wonder why people don't tell him not to sit here. Why is this okay? I bet you if a black GS-15 sat at this table and started nodding off we would be reprimanded for days to come but not Jasper. Jasper is a malnourished looking white dude who can come sit at the table throw out his two cents every so often and fall back asleep.

I am brought back to the present moment when Lt Gen Frank speaks.

"Great job running this down Ava."

"Thanks Sir."

"You are proposing we look at realigning some of our funding for this next FYDP to better support our flightline maintenance."

"Yes Sir."

I should say I am also equally impressed that I gave an entire briefing and had an entirely different thought process going on in my head. That is most definitely a sign that I have mastered this bureaucratic slavery and it's time for me to move on. This happened back at Tinker Air Force Base as well. I once gave a briefing having never looked at the slides my boss prepared for me. I glided through the entire briefing with a bunch of two-star generals and didn't skip a beat and got praised for my presentation.

Today I'm having another Black Excellence moment as I've nailed this briefing while in deep wonderment about the Jaspers in this place and yet an entirely different set of words are coming out of my mouth. Yep, I've mastered this shit.

"Yeah, so here's the problem with your proposal. The Hill asked if we need more funding for similar requirements."

"Yes, I am aware of that."

"You saw the request from The Hill asking us why we weren't requesting more funding. This is the same as their question the other week about our fighter fleet budget."

No shit.

"I did but we don't need more money. We just need to realign our current funding.

"If we do that, we will look like we don't need additional funding."

"Yes, that is correct."

And here comes the bullshit. This is like Groundhog Day meets broken Stepford Wife chip. They don't hear you. They're on replay and no matter what you do, you can't reprogram them.

"I think the best way forward is to write a response highlighting where we need more funding."

"Um hum."

"There just isn't another option."

"There's the option of being truthful. How about we respond by saying we manage our budget correctly with subject matter expertise; therefore, we are not seeking an increase to our budget. This is the same response I proposed the other week when we had the fighter fleet question but unfortunately my suggestion wasn't used. Perhaps today it will be."

"Ava, really?"

"Really Sir."

"That's possible," mumbles Jasper.

I wish I could be white for just a day and see how these people live.

"Sir, with all due respect. I just can't do that."

"Why not? Have we missed the suspense?"

"No, we would be lying and I can't do that."

"Sure, you can."

Lt Gen Frank is laughing. He is either amused with himself, me or has finally lost it altogether. His face is turning red and he is wiping tears of laughter from his face.

"I can't! That's hilarious! I know you're now some Zen Master but I didn't think that made you the ethics queen."

"Actually, Sir this is something we all should be mindful of and we are required to take annual ethics training."

"You know what I mean. Well, if you can't do it, have someone on your team to do it but an honest answer will not grow our budget."

I now want to throw something at Lt Gen Frank.

"Fine Sir. I'll have something for you by close of business."

I see Lt Col Insecure grinning from ear to ear. Perhaps I should have said since Mike did such a great job falsifying our requirements for the fighter fleet, he should draft up another bullshit response for this tasker.

"Perfect and excellent briefing! You haven't lost your touch! You all know I've known Ava since she was knee high to a briefing slide! She's so terrific at giving briefings they had her brief other folks' projects back at Tinker. The Briefing Lady is what they called you, right?"

"Yep."

Lt Gen Frank gets up to leave and the room rises to attention.

"Carry on. Oh, and Ava, I miss the old you."

The thing is this is the old me. I've never agreed with any of the shit we do around here, I've just never really said anything. This is my first time pushing back with the option of honesty but I knew it was a failed solution from the start. There's no way in hell we're going to pass on receiving additional funding.

I bet with all that money saved we could go back to the old retirement program and if that were the case I could retire today but instead they keep us here until we're damn near dead. And when it's all over you get a fraction of the money you were making and let's hope you stashed a lot away in your TSP (Thrift Savings Plan) or some other form of savings or investments. In either case before I completely spiral into a place that I've digressed into depression I'll stop now.

I stack up my papers, turn off the computer and the projector screen. The room is empty now and as I look around, I feel the hollowness around me.

27

Big Red

The more I learn about the power of manifesting the more I enjoy bringing amazing things into my life! Today I am at the Jeep dealership buying a Firecracker Red Jeep Wrangler Unlimited. It's not that I don't love my baby Range Rover but it was never me, it was Dan. It was me falling in line with what he thought was best for me; an image he thought I should be projecting to the world.

The truth is I've longed to own a Jeep for years but convinced myself that it wasn't a practical vehicle. I've concluded that anything I drive is practical since it's me with two very tiny dogs and so today I am purchasing Big Red. That's her name and I absolutely love her.

About 30 days ago I decided I wanted a red Jeep. Every time I went to the garage and walked towards my baby Range Rover I saw a bright shiny red Jeep. I would open the door to the Range Rover and climb inside as if I was climbing up into a Jeep and then proceed to drive it as if I was in a Jeep and not a crossover SUV. Fast forward to earlier this morning about 1 AM. I had just finished working on my novel and decided to peruse the certified pre-owned selections and to my excitement there was a fully loaded special edition Sahara with low miles for exactly $1000 less then I wanted to pay.

This Jeep is a sign I am moving in the right direction. Why can't I do this with other stuff, like getting the hell out of here or spending more time with my man? I'm guessing it's the negative energy around the strong desire for those things that keeps them at bay. With the Jeep and other smaller things, it just comes because I'm almost indifferent to them happening. Not that I don't want them but I know I am at peace with or without them. I need to be this way about everything. My life will be good and will be great when I let go, believe, trust and get about living my life. I'm sure I'll forget this very sound advice I am receiving from my Spirit Team in the near future and then remember again but I do hope it begins to stick sooner verses later.

"You're all set Ms. McClure. Do you need assistance getting your other vehicle home?"

The salesman, Jeremy, has been a joy to work with. He's at best 25, tall and extremely slender. His blue eyes appear to be drowning in the sea as he looks extremely tired.

"Actually, I plan to sell it. Can you follow me to Auto Trades in Woodbridge?"

"I sure can! I'd love to get behind the wheel of a Range Rover!"

"Great, thanks!"

Jeremy hands me the keys to Big Red and I pull out the keys for the Evoque and hand them to him.

I am driving slowly to Auto Trades as it occurred to me once we left the dealership that Jeremy does look very tired and I need him to get my car to Auto Trades without incident. I am also thinking about Lucas. He will be with me tomorrow for my biopsy and I am grateful for him taking time for me.

Moving into his place has not yet happened and neither of us have discussed it in the last couple of weeks. I think we both know it was a rushed decision and are at peace with how things are going for us. The fact that I have a key to his place and I let myself in whenever I come over is enough for us. Also, the fact that I gave him a key to my place and he didn't ask me why since I am supposed to be moving out and into his place is another a sign we are on the same page. I see our key exchange as promise keys though I am aware we do need to acknowledge where things are with us. I don't want the unspoken to be our way of communicating as a lot can be misunderstood this way.

Every day I am stronger in my self-love and awareness of my soul's purpose and there is great comfort in this. I am able to fully relax in Lucas' love and respect for me and this feels like light years from any place I've ever known.

I still think about our cultural differences. I recall the looks and hateful comments from people most of whom were black men upset to see me with a white man back in Oklahoma. I remember thinking if only they knew how pro black I was but you couldn't tell it from seeing me hugged up with a white man at a restaurant or movie. The truth, at least my version of the truth, was there were no black men around for me to date at least not in the circles I traveled in. I went to bars and rocked out to punk bands as if I hadn't spent four years nestled deep in my blackness at Alabama State University. And, when I first moved to Oklahoma City in 1995 there wasn't even an R&B radio station. If it were not for BET, I wouldn't have had a clue as to what was going on in black culture.

I don't know where the worst place to be in an interracial relationship is. I do know the story of Richard and Mildred Loving back in the 50s and for me it was Oklahoma City in the late 90s and early 2000s. It was brutal, but I mustered through. I got told things like I should just turn white like Michael Jackson did if that's what I wanted. And one night at 2 AM as the club was letting out two black guys were appalled to see me kiss and say goodnight to my boyfriend who was a blond haired blue-eyed hottie in my opinion. What was funny was I couldn't figure out why they were at this bar because it was totally a white peoples bar. I asked them and they had no response so I began cussing them out. Drunk, my words slurred as I rattled off insults that surprisingly embarrassed them. It took my friend to calm me down and escort me to my sexy little sports car. As she drove off, I rolled down the window and gave them a few more choice words.

In either case this matters to me but not enough to end things with Lucas. I know I owe it to myself to learn from this relationship and to continue to grow and nurture myself. Truthfully, it's like I am in my early twenties and just discovering the world of dating as an adult only this time I am doing it with the awareness of who I am and what I want. Lucas and I are moving slow and steady and this feels good.

I pull into the parking lot of Auto Trades and park. Jeremy parks next to me. I look over at the Evoque and smile.

"Goodbye Dan," I say as I hop out of the Jeep.

"Jeremy, thanks so much! This shouldn't take long so I should have you back at the dealership in no time."

"Oh no worries, I'm happy to wait. I could use the break."

Jeremy looks as though he could curl up and take a nap in the parking lot.

"You do seem tired."

"Partied hard last night", he says with a yawn.

"I remember those days."

I smile and walk inside.

The process was quick and I had Jeremy back at the dealership within an hour. I am now driving home and feeling tired from the events of the day. My phone rings and Lucas' name appears on the screen.

"Hey, how was your day?"

"It was great, busy but great. How about yours?"

"My day was fantastic! I am driving my new Jeep!"

"What! Yeah! I am so glad you now have what you want baby!"

"Thank you, sweetie!"

"I'm calling to ensure you are going to be resting the rest of today. I know it's just a biopsy but I want you to have a nice quiet night and only think good positive thoughts."

"You are so thoughtful. Yes, sweetie I am almost home. Just going to take the girls for a walk then dinner followed by chilling out with some meditation time."

"Perfect. I will meet you there tomorrow, my love."

"Okay, thank you so much baby, I appreciate you."

I end the call as I am driving into the garage. Tomorrow will be a good day. I am healthy and I don't have time for anything but for this to be true.

28
Biopsy Day

I'm feeling peaceful and my rose quartz and amethyst crystals are in my purse. This isn't my first rodeo and it quite possibly won't be my last with biopsies but it is my first biopsy since I started my journey into the world of alternative healing, manifestation, and an overall deeper since of self and soul connection.

The elevator door opens and I step out to see Lucas dressed in khakis and a button down blue shirt chatting with a doctor. I shouldn't be surprised he beat me here since he works at this hospital.

"Ava!"

I walk over and Lucas gives me a hug and kiss.

"Ava, this is Doctor Aaron Jones. We did our residency together."

I extend my hand to greet a handsome black man who stands at the same height as Lucas.

"Hello, it's nice to meet you."

"You as well. Lucas has shared so many wonderful things about you."

I smile at Lucas who pulls me close by my waist.

"Awe, that's nice to know. If you would excuse me, I'm going to check in."

"Of course," they say in unison.

I walk over to the receptionist and sign in. As I walk back to Lucas and Aaron, I can't help but check for a ring. Nope, not wearing one. I am sure though this handsome mocha man is dating someone. I'll have to ask Lucas. Maybe Aaron would be a good match for one of my girlfriends. I can't think of one of them that wouldn't think he was handsome and Sheryl would definitely take interest because of his doctor status which is actually a good reason not to play match maker at least not for her.

I could use this brief moment to ponder why I didn't meet a handsome black doctor but I won't because I am in love with this handsome Latino doctor who took time out of his day to be here with me. Though the fact that I just thought about having that thought says that I did just think about it. I guess that's natural. What's important is I am relaxing into love and slowly letting the race thing go.

"I've got to run. It was nice to meet you."

"You too Dr. Jones."

"Aaron, please."

I smile as Lucas takes my hand.

"We were saying the four of us need to go out sometime."

"Yes, Angela would love to double date."

"I would love to meet her!"

That answers that question.

"Let's make it happen soon," says Aaron.

"Yes, we will," says Lucas.

Aaron heads down the hall and Lucas guides me to the waiting area.

We are silent as I rest my head on his shoulder.

A few minutes later I speak.

"I don't know when the best time is to bring this up so I thought I'd just do it now."

"You mean the great key exchange."

I laugh.

"Okay so we're on the same page?"

"I was a bit quick with my move in with me proposal and you were so kind to agree."

"I want to be with you and living together would've given us more time together."

"I want to be with you and asking you to move in with me was my way of showing you how committed I am to us."

"I am committed to us too. We're moving along at a nice pace don't you think?"

"I do."

Lucas kisses me on the forehead and then on the lips.

"I thought I'd see you looking all doctor'ish in your scrubs or at least your lab coat."

"Ah, if I were I couldn't or at least I shouldn't kiss you like this."

Lucas's lips are brushing against mine and I feel my heart beating faster. He kisses me gently on the lips as I hear my name being called.

"Ava McClure."

I stand up and give Lucas a peck on the lips. He grabs my hand and smiles. I smile back and walk towards the nurse who called my name.

I am once again freezing as I wait for the procedure to begin. Maybe they can provide blankets while you wait. It looks as though the nurse has read my mind as she walks over to a cabinet and pulls out a blanket.

"This should help."

"Thank you."

She smiles as she drapes the blanket over me. A few minutes later two doctors enter the room. The process is quick and painless. Numb my breast, wait a few minutes. While we wait, they explain what they are going to do which is make a small incision in my breast, remove a sample of the mass and put a marker on the remaining part of it so they can easily find it in the future.

I'm dressed and heading back to the waiting area. Before I open the door to exit, I see Lucas through the window. He is such a kind man. God, you have truly blessed me with a wonderful thoughtful soul. I am realizing in this moment my concerns about our differences are rooted in the hurtful remarks I remember from years ago. I am surrendering my concerns and embracing this relationship one hundred percent.

I open the door and Lucas looks up. He stands and we walk towards each other.

"How was it?"

"Easy breezy. Plus, I had my rose quartz and amethyst with me."

"What do they do?"

"Their metaphysical properties are known to support love, health and healing."

I opt to keep my explanation simple as I can see Lucas is confused.

"Like the crystals in my apartment."

"Oh, I thought those were for decoration like people wear stones in jewelry."

"They can also be decorative while doing the healing they do."

It is occurring to me that I haven't shared anything about crystals with Lucas. He knows I meditate, take yoga classes and I've mentioned the lightworker and Reiki classes but I've not shared my deeper exploration into alternative healing. It's something I mention in passing probably because I'm still learning and am unsure about so much of it. I will be sure to discuss it with him. He of all people would have some interest in alternative health.

"Ready for lunch?"

"I am. Where are we going?"

"The cafeteria."

"Really!"

"I'm kidding! You don't want to eat there, do you?"

"I am happy with whatever since it means we get to spend a little bit more time together today."

"Okay, cafeteria it is but be ready for more talking than eating as everyone will want to meet you."

"I'd love to meet your colleagues."

The elevator doors open and we enter. You see Ava, this is what an adult relationship feels like.

29
Vomit

For the first time in my 22-year career I got violently ill today at work. I was in the food court with Jamie having breakfast and I kept getting more and more nauseous. I knew I had come in with a pretty bad sinus headache and the pressure from it being 96% humidity this morning was weighing me down but I didn't expect to get sick. We parted ways and I headed to the pharmacy to pick up something for my headache. I waited patiently for the pharmacist who was extremely busy because I knew only a decongestant would relieve the pain. As I waited the nausea got worse. Finally, it was my turn. I was barely able to pay before I bolted out of the store and ran to the nearest restroom.

I then experienced a 20-to-30-minute episode of vomiting. I have never in my entire career vomited at work. I would like to think it was the weather and the sinus headache but I know it's more. It is because I don't want to be here. Sitting in the food court, chatting with Jamie felt complacent. It felt as though there was no end in sight even though I am powering through my novel. It's the hollowness of this place, the dark hollowness that is sweeping over me. I am losing my California vibe even though I am still meditating every day. This building and the entire Beltway is like the Bermuda Triangle, only everyone is living in the bowels of the triangle like an underworld. Going to California was me escaping and now it's like I am hovering right above the point that will suck me back in and I'll be damn if I let it.

The working title for my novel is Illusions. This feels right because all I ever did until my recent return was fake the funk. My official photo looks like I love what I do and love this place. To drill into my mind would be the unmasking of so many lies. Lies I've told myself, lies told to me by my parents, lies that led me here in the first place. The cover will be me naked in chains. I thought it only fitting since the premise of the book is me feeling enslaved. Of course, Ms. Sally helped me to see I am the master who put myself in chains something the character will also discover by the end of the novel series.

30
Results

I'm in a makeshift office half-dressed and freezing as I do whenever I am here. Has anyone thought that bringing a person to a cold sterile makeshift office and having them wait half naked for a long period of time to get their biopsy results is not a good idea -perhaps quite nerve racking. I don't feel nerve racked but rather calm but I am sure most folks are not and I am wondering where do men go for biopsy results? Do they come here for 3D ultrasounds and sonograms?

I'm fine is what she's saying -just fibroadenoma masses are quite common in young women. I like the young women part. I am halfway listening as I can't quite explain it but I knew I was fine. I will call Lucas and let him know. I am still romanticizing the day I came in for the biopsy. Him being here waiting for me and us having lunch afterwards and meeting his colleagues goes down in history as a delightful date.

I took the opportunity to start explaining alternative healing practices in more detail to Lucas that day to which he looked at me smiled and said, "I am a tangible kind of guy."

My rebuttal was simple.

"Before this there was nothing else." I said with my arms wide open to show the totality of the hospital and western medicine.

"There were herbs and flower remedies which I do believe work to varying degrees. What you are explaining is not that. You are talking about witchcraft and magic."

"It's neither of those things. It's God. And crystals are powerful."

"Look, I get the placebo effect. Doctors have studied it but it's not real science."

My look of disappointment seemed to shatter Lucas.

"Oh, now sweetie. Hey, if it helps people that's all that matters. I love that you've found a hobby that can help you take a break from writing."

At this point I was speechless but I didn't feel I was knowledgeable enough to counter his argument so I let it go. We then met a host of his colleagues and soon I'd forgotten about our discussion.

31
Hoochie Mamas

Hoochie makes its way into the Pentagon every day and age is not a limiting factor. I think I've seen it all throughout my years here. From fishnets to see through linen with hot pink underwear it's all been done. I don't however understand why these women choose to dress so inappropriately and I don't know what they do here. I've never worked with anyone who dresses this way and I interface with tons of people so I'm always curious when I see them in the halls as to where in the hell do they work and what do they do. This will quite possibly remain a mystery that'll be with me when I die.

I'm waiting on my latte and typing up this note about the hoochies on my phone for my novel when I see an older black man walking by brushing his very large mustache with what appears to be a brush one would use to shine shoes. The other day I saw a white man collecting bottle caps in the food court and this morning I passed a man in the hall dressed in jeans a blazer and goloshes. We here at Shawshank don't typically wear jeans even on Fridays and it's a bright sunny day so I was not understanding the goloshes. Last summer during a 90 degree day, I saw an Asian man in his flight jacket who was clearly insecure. I say this because there can't be any good reason for wearing your flight jacket in the dead of summer unless you are doubling down on ensuring everyone knows you're a pilot. This place gets stranger by the day and people say the folks in LA are weird.

I'm getting further and further removed from my time in California. It's hard to believe this time two years ago I was starting to pack the house I was renting and looking for a place to stay in Santa Monica. Why do I still miss it so much? I was reborn there or perhaps born. I know I was broken open there.

Nala just announced a few weeks ago she's moving to Belize. She's leaving LA and here I am dreaming of my return. Amy said my Ascended Masters said I could return and I am holding on to that just without the definitive timeline I had placed on myself when I came back here last year. I also know I can't be like Moses and die in the desert a.k.a. Shawshank. I know God called me back here to lead and be an inspiration for others and unlike Moses I have to get to the promised land. I know that once I am there I will be of even more support for others.

32

Giving Away My Rocks

Today I gave away my rose quartz and blue onyx crystals at a going away luncheon to a coworker. I was sharing with our small group that I use them to keep myself calm at work and they were joking about one of our coworkers being extremely over the top with drama and how they thought throwing them was a better option than sometimes placing them in my jacket pocket. Jim, the lucky guy who is leaving Shawshank asked if he could hold them. I handed them to him and he started rolling them around in his hand.

I watched him transform as he slowly rolled the crystals around. Jim is the guy who is just kind of there. Mad at the world but not doing anything to change his experience. As he kept rolling them, he began to smile and he seemed far more relaxed. This happened in a matter of minutes. I could tell he didn't want to part with them and I told him he could hang onto them for the rest of the day. Before the end of the luncheon, I told him he could keep them.

"Okay, 'cause I wasn't giving these rocks back," he said jokingly and with ease.

Later in the afternoon I gave another co-worker my Chakra bracelet. Sandy was sharing a host of things with me and each one seem to lower my vibration as she continued on. As she spoke, all I could think of was I have to give her my Chakra bracelet. I don't want to seem weird or crazy or act like I'm better than others but she needs this bracelet. It's telling me to give it to her so I slide it off my wrist and I said, "Take this."

Sandy laughed as she was with me at the luncheon where I talked about the healing power of crystals but she held out her hand to receive it. I explained Chakras and each of the tiny little crystals that represented the seven Chakras. I told her not to worry if she didn't remember what each crystal was or how they supported her. I knew if she just put the bracelet on and didn't think about it things would calm down for her.

What struck me though as I was walking home was that I had just given away two crystals and a Chakra bracelet that I had obtained in Santa Monica. Precious items I had carried with me towards the end of my fellowship and back across the country. These were part of my balance and peace and it's not to say I don't still need support with being balanced and at peace but I knew in those moments Jim and Sandy needed them more than I did.

When I got home, I said a prayer for them after my meditation and sent peace, love and tranquility which I'm sure they received.

I felt good. I felt I was being the lightworker Amy says I am.

I feel like I've come to a place of understanding about why am still here in this job that I so greatly hate; back to 100% of where I was nine years ago when I first moved here; back to the exact same office, back to the exact same weird culture of people who are just as freaking crazy as they were then. It's not because of this job though I do have to do it every day. It's because of the lives I'm touching. My Spirit Team led me to support Jim and then Sandy. Both times felt easy, nurturing and part of my purpose.

I am now reflecting on how much I have been sharing. Not just the crystals I gave away today but with a host of other encounters throughout these past months. I don't say much, just what I intuitively feel I should and for all I know they might think I'm a quack but I know they feel better. They laugh a little bit more and my presence in this office has lifted the entire spirit of this directorate. Plus, the meditation and breathwork practices with my team have been transformative.

I cried many tears. I sobbed as I thought about how much I hated the idea of returning to the DMV. And to come back to the same office I hired into nine years ago. Nine years ago, there was nothing I could do to help anyone; there was nothing I could do to help myself. I was lost, confused, and running away from a bad relationship, running away from hurt and rejection. Nine years ago, I was a baby. It seem like a lifetime ago and yet it feels like it was yesterday. I remember moving here so vividly. I am dictating this on my laptop right now in the same apartment building I first moved into nine years ago.

I kept asking God why. Why are you taking me back full circle? But it's not, it is a new beginning. God blessed me with a great man in my life something I will be forever grateful for. He has ascended me to a place in my life where I can be of service to others in the darkness and shadows of Shawshank.

I knew I needed to come back here the day I was crying on Ventura Boulevard. There was a deep-rooted part of me that understood there was something that needed to be done here. I thought it was writing my novel and most definitely it is but in addition to writing one of the best damn novels anyone will ever read it was to give back to Shawshank. This crappy, awful nasty place to work with insecure humans drenched in egotism. We play defense every day. We plan wars. We strategize things that are not pleasant. Down every hallway there's nothing but pictures of bombers, tankers, fighters, tanks, and submarines -all used in war. We walk through the halls haunted by heroes - by the memories of our fallen soldiers and dedications to wars and battles. And not to mention the bloodstains from 9/11, it's corridor and memorial. How can anyone feel any level of peace in this place without having a healthy meditation practice at a minimum?

The question is do they know how dark and hollow they are? I am guessing they don't. If you had told me I was dark and hollow prior to my time in California, I would have said you were crazy. Unhappy here because of the *Groundhog Day* effect and calling it Shawshank because I felt trapped as I wanted to be a writer but not because I was constantly absorbing death and destruction.

Maybe some know and they compartmentalize it, which is still unhealthy. In either case, I see how I am to be of service while I am here and I will do my part to bring love and light to this place.

33

GS-15

I accepted a GS-15 position in a new directorate which is not located at Shawshank. I am not remotely interested in anything this office supports but it makes sense financially. The extra money will allow me to save more so I can exit Shawshank as soon as possible.

I also know it's time to leave this office and spread love and light into other parts of this abyss. It's my understanding of how I am continuing to step more into my calling.

I am engulfed in a strange sense of sadness as my time at Shawshank comes to an end. The place I cried about returning to is now the place I'm sad to leave. My new job is out of the building and I'm being paroled again. Only this time not to sunny Santa Monica but dreary Maryland. In either case I'm being released. I should feel elated about this but somehow Shawshank has become my home, again. I fought like crazy not to return from California and now just one year back in this place my heart sinks a little at the thought of saying goodbye. The majority of my friends are here, plus the familiar faces of people I've seen for years in the halls and at various locations – food court, pharmacy, bank. I never bothered to know most of their names but we know each other just the same. The water delivery guy, the custodians, the folks that work at Burger King and Subway.

I'm sad to be leaving? Can't be. Scared about what lies ahead for the new job? No. I know God has me fully equipped for whatever they have in store for me. I'm not sad to move on to the new job but sad to leave this place. Sad to leave this office where just the other day I asked a co-worker who was stressing out if she'd ever tried sound healing. Though she and another co-worker busted into laughter and I replied - oops I went too Zen on you, it's now my home. But they too will move on, the military will PCS (Permanent Change of Station) the civilians will find another office to serve time in and the faces in this space will change. But the culture will not the Air Force'ism will remain the Groundhog Day'ness will be here always. It's actually rather comforting.

I am tossing a few things into a box when Ted returns to the office.

"I've decided you can't leave us."

"Really," I laugh.

"We need you. **Your** don't give a shit attitude is so refreshing and honestly entertaining to watch when you piss Mike off with it. Plus, I've got some big decisions to make and I was hoping to have you here as I sort out my life."

I've been in this office just one year and Ted has aged even more. It appears he has gone from whipped to dead like the shell of a soul hanging on who is ready to transition to the soul realm. I take a deep breath and smile.

"All you have to do is practice the breathing and meditation I taught you. I know I'm going to sound like Buddha to you right now but the answers all live within you. They are right here, remember?"

I point to my Third Eye Chakra; Ted smiles and mimics my gesture.

"And, what's even more cool is **meditation brings a higher sense of understanding, a higher sense of awareness.**"

"You know you don't belong here."

"I think I do, for a little while longer at least."

I reach out and shake Ted's hand then pick up my box. I take one last look around and head out the door. I feel good. I can pass on little nuggets to people everywhere I go and I think there's a lot of nuggets that need to be passed out in my new office. It's a Cyber and Intel operation and lord knows there's enough secrets and covert operations to drive a person mad.

Thank you, God, for letting me be the light for some people in this world and thank you God that my writing will do that as well. I can't leave yet as I understand that I have more light to bring to this dark world. I won't touch all 26000 people that work in the Pentagon but I might touch 20 and they might touch 20 more and so on and so on and maybe just maybe this place will get a little bit brighter.

34
Alone at the Kennedy Center

I am having a dateless night at the Kennedy Center. Lucas and I were supposed to be celebrating his promotion to chief of surgery and my promotion to GS-15 but he was asked to consult on a case in Detroit.

Being the thoughtful man he is, he bought a ticket for me to see the National Symphony Orchestra so I'll still have something to do tonight. Honestly going alone although I've done it a few times in the past including when he and I first met is not feeling so great. Lucas has been incredibly busy with his new position plus more shmoozing than before with potential donors. I know this is the life of a woman dating a surgeon but sometimes it's a bit lonely.

I was indifferent about being there when I arrived but when the usher opened the door to show me to my seat something in that very moment changed. He opened the door and I walked through the sitting area something I'd never done before, something I had not thought about existing. Then he open a second door and showed me to my seat which was the center box; a location I thought was reserved for the elite of D.C. The view was breathtaking and although I was alone, I felt Lucas' love surrounding me.

In those brief seconds of me walking through those doors I was reminded again of the beautiful gift Lucas gives me and it's his love. His love was expressed through his desire to ensure I enjoyed the evening and his thoughtfulness in selecting incredible seats with a beautiful view.

After the opening act there was a short break and I used it as an opportunity to go to the restroom. When I came back and walked through the first door, I started thanking God for Lucas and our love for each other. And I acknowledged to God and myself that yes indeed I am worthy. I am worthy of love and happiness. I am worthy of opening my heart to trust. Yes, I deserve this. I deserve to be with a man who loves me so much that he would go out of his way to give me such an amazing night. I felt myself returning to the open heart that I had the night we first met and dismissing my thoughts that we were drifting apart.

35

Illusions

I'm a published author for the second time! I am once again **at the bookstore** signing copies of my novel for Mary. She said it's a nice added touch to have a few copies signed by the author for purchase. I am over the moon excited as I sign one copy then the next. Mary seems to be enjoying the moment as she takes pictures of me signing the books.

"Congratulations on your second book!"

"Thanks, part one down and two more to go."

"I like your idea of turning it into a book series verses one novel. You know there are a lot of studies that say the average person doesn't have the attention span to read a five-hundred-page book anymore."

"Yes, I've read some of those studies and it got me to thinking about the series. Plus, so much of this character is me that I feel I can be more fluid with how her world evolves by writing one book at a time."

"It's perfect and might I say, it was very bold of you to use your picture on the cover. I mean we cropped it so there's nothing showing but still this is you naked in chains."

"It's part of me freeing myself."

Mary nods her head in agreement.

I pick up one of the books and smile. Yep, that's me naked in chains with a picture of Shawshank superimposed in the background. I kept my working title of Illusions. The first book in the *Illusions* series is *Enslaved* which will be followed by at least two more books *Enlightened* and *Emancipated.* I am already halfway through Enlightened and I plan to write Emancipated during my last few months as it should be ceremoniously published days after I turn in my badge and never look back at Shawshank.

For now, I will take the advice of the folks back in Hollywood and start sending my book out to those I met out there and others who may be interested in my story. I am feeling the chains break and I think about how well my novel series will be received. It's time for me to tell my truth and this first book is just the beginning.

36
New Home

Today is moving day. After being back for two years I decided it was time to purchase a home. My decision to do so was strictly based on not giving the government any more money than I had to and not having mortgage interest to itemize was starting to tilt me into the you owe after filing your taxes category.

This condo is my third home purchase and my first practical home purchase. My other two homes in Oklahoma were dream homes. This is a necessity. I am though blessed to have the equity it will generate over time. I know my lack of excitement is related to Lucas and me deciding not to live together. Purchasing my own home says more than tax write off. It says we are nowhere close to moving in together and honestly, I don't think we ever will be.

Lucas has been M.I.A. a lot since he was promoted to chief of surgery. I understand the management responsibilities and extra hours or at least I think I do because I watch *Grey's Anatomy*. But it's more than the time apart for us. I have now become a Reiki Master Teacher, Sound Healer, Ayurveda Teacher and have started an alternative healing business. My client roster has grown rather quickly and I love being of service in this way. I still recall having no idea what Reiki was or why Amy thought I was a healer and now I am a Life Coach/Spiritual Counselor/Reiki Master helping others to obtain inner peace and free themselves from their mental plantations. Most of my clients are government employees and contractors along with some military members and this makes me relatable to them. I am in their shoes and I have discovered ways to rise above the dreaded Groundhog Days.

Lucas, who has said on more than one occasion he believes in the tangible, is less than encouraging and thinks it's all a bunch of woo woo. When I told him my psychic abilities were getting stronger from my meditation practice, he couldn't hold it together and burst out laughing. Needless to say, my feelings were hurt.

"Ava, you can't go around telling people things like this. You sound foolish."

"It's not foolish. It's real."

"It's not."

"How do you know?"

"I just do. None of what you do is real sweetie and the fact that people pay to spend time with you for your services is an insult to the medical profession."

"You know, there are doctors who practice both Western and Eastern medicine."

"I know. I think those that do are trying to cash in on this new wave of crazy."

"It's not new or crazy. Before there was Western medicine, this is all there was. Ayurveda is a five-thousand-year-old healing system."

"That is not scientifically backed."

"There are many parts of it that is to include the benefits of meditation."

"You're wrong."

"How am I wrong when there are studies that validate this? And let's not forget that I healed from my hysterectomy a few months ago using only peppermint oil and sleeping with my rose quartz crystal. I didn't have the prescriptions filled for those pain meds."

"It's nonsense."

"I think it's going to be hard for our relationship if you are so put off by what I do as part of my soul's purpose."

"Ava, you have a good job. You make great money and you have published some books. Why does this need to be part of what you do?"

"This is who I am. My next book in my novel series will show the character learning many of these practices. I want to enlighten others on ways they can expand spiritually, emotionally and physically."

"Well, don't expect me to introduce you to people and tell them you do this stuff. I will be the laughingstock among my colleagues. You know that stuff is nothing more than the placebo effect."

I had nothing else to say after that as this was now a Groundhog Day discussion with Lucas. All I could think was this understanding of how he feels about alternative healing is a red flag. Or perhaps another red flag. Since his promotion he's become more arrogant and dismissive as if he is too good for me. I can see how dating a government employee is not the most impressive thing considering how we are typically stereotyped as lazy but we've been together for a couple of years now and he knows me and my work ethic and the billions of dollars I manage. Albeit I am not the go-getter I used to be but to him I appear to be a hard working slave of the Pentagon.

It could also be God giving me an easy out. While I have relaxed into this relationship with Lucas, I still yearn to date a black man. I still want to have my strong black man. The man that can relate to my struggles as a black woman. The man I can have deep discussions with about our people and how we need to uplift each other. The man who I can walk into an African Centered event with and not feel like I have to explain everything to. The man I can go to a black movie with and he gets the jokes and the message.

I recall going to see *The Best Man* and *Brown Sugar* with one of the white men I was dating in Oklahoma. Beyond the judgy looks from the black folks it was frustrating to watch these movies with him. Circumstances about the characters he didn't understand, jokes he didn't get. I spent the entire time translating for him instead of enjoying the movies.

I know the answer will come as to what lies ahead for us and when it does, I will be okay with it as I've know from the beginning that this relationship was part of my healing journey. I did on some level hope it could be more but I understand if that is not how this story ends.

37
Ecuador

During the first year of living in the DMV I went to the National Portrait Gallery to see the presidents' portraits. I was curious to see George W. Bush's portrait as news reports were making a big deal of his portrait because he was not wearing a suit and he wasn't in an official "posing" position. So, on an extremely cold winter day I found myself staring at his portrait with a smile on my face. Rebel was what came to mind. After delighting in the militancy of President Bush, I wandered into another exhibit of movie posters and reveled at the poster for the movie *Carmen*. How fitting I thought as she too was somewhat of a rebel. I wanted to be a rebel but at the time I was deeply enslaved in my life as a federal employee and new to Shawshank.

I then drifted off to a very large hallway where there was a statue called Nirvana. The statue seemed to be at least ten feet tall. There was a bench that was about twenty feet away from it. I walked over and took a seat. I sat there marveling at this being whose head was cloaked and had no face yet it stared at me and I stared back. The plaque stated the name, Nirvana and noted this is a place of just being – neither happy nor sad. I was 34 at the time and was as lost as ever. I think back on that statue today and I now understand Nirvana. I get there quite often during my meditations and I am in this state now as I perform Reiki in this quaint village in Ecuador.

I am here with Nala. She's hosting a meditation retreat and offered free room and board for someone who could be her apprentice. I sent her an email and volunteered to give Reiki to everyone in exchange for the free room and board and she was happy for me to share my gifts this week. I am thankful as I am working to save as much as possible to free myself from Shawshank in a few years.

This week has been spectacular. I have connected with the other workshop attendees and have given sessions to the attendees plus those in the village. I've also spent an incredible amount of time at the beach. And the views! I do the sessions at the top of a massive treehouse. The people relax on a yoga mat with crystals aligned along their bodies and essential oils infusing their skin and the air. Standing above them my view is the ocean in the distance. To be here giving Reiki in such a sacred place is beyond anything I could have imagined. Four years ago, I was in search of something to support me and now I've traveled to a foreign country by myself to be with this loving group of people and be a vessel of healing for them.

This has also been a nice break from Lucas who rolled his eyes at the idea of me coming here. When I told him about the living situation that we would be living in huts showering outdoors and using compost toilets he gave me the most disgusting look. He asked why can't this year's retreat be someplace domestic like last year's which was in Rancho Santa Fe. I felt the need to point out that he is from Argentina.

"And," was his reply.

"You are from South America."

"From a rich civilized country."

"So, Ecuador is not good enough for you?"

"Or you Ava. Why in the world do you feel the need to go do missionary work?"

"It's not missionary work it's a retreat in a village that was built purposefully to be ecofriendly and minimalistic."

"Why don't you skip this trip and I will take you on an amazing vacation to Argentina. We haven't taken a vacation in a while. It will be exciting. You can meet my family and practice your Spanish."

"I've committed to going and I'm not going to back out. I'm leaving in three days."

"Fine but don't call me if something goes or awry over there because all I'm going to do is say I told you so."

"I wouldn't expect anything more of you."

Before Lucas could respond the lights were dimming in the movie theater. We didn't discuss it further after the show. We rode back to my place in silence and while he did spend the night it was a passionless sleepover.

He is correct in that he cannot share this part of me with his colleagues but it isn't because they wouldn't get it it's because he's embarrassed by me. Lucas needs to be with another doctor or perhaps an attorney or perhaps the old Ava who simply doesn't exist anymore. To be honest she was already gone when we met and what has emerged since we started dating is someone I sometimes don't recognize but I love the hell out of her.

Lucus loves to tell people I work at the Pentagon and that I manage billions of dollars for the Air Force. I love to tell people that I am a Reiki Master Teacher and I serve as a vessel of God's beautiful healing energy. I know it's time to end things with him as the distance we've drifted apart feels like the distance from the Santa Monica Beach to the Potomac River. Even more truthfully, I'm just realizing how different we are. Being here this week, being in my element has helped me to see this clearly though the signs were there on our first date.

This week I have been free. Like that Nirvana statue I just am. I don't feel any sadness when I accept things must end with Lucas. It's just something that must occur. I've learned a lot and grown a lot from this relationship and for the first time I felt what others feel when they say they are in love. But just like the saying goes reasons, seasons, and lifetimes. Lucas has been both a reason and a season.

It is the last day of the retreat and we are taking part in a Cacao ceremony. It is a ceremony of gratitude and openness. As I sit in this circle with the others I am thinking about my security clearance. I have no clue if Cacao is on the drug list though somehow, I don't think it would be since it's the source of chocolate and today I don't give a shit. If I return to work next week and get randomly drug tested and this shows up as a drug because in its raw form you can get blissed out, fuck it. It's time for me to live in the moment. There are many reasons why I am planning my escape from Shawshank and this is one of them. I don't want to live under their rules. I don't want to report who in the hell I spoke to while visiting Ecuador. I'm not free. Not free to enjoy my life. Some might think it's a small sacrifice when we make such wonderful salaries but for me it's stifling.

As I take the last sip from my cup I smile and think about peeing in a cup next week. I am so tickled I'm laughing. Others have begun dancing and singing. I see Nala dancing and I float over to her.

"Thank you for this week. I needed it greatly!"

"You're welcome. We needed you this week. Everything works just as it should."

"Indeed."

"You know, everyone loved their sessions with you. They said they felt so much lighter; at a place of peace they've never experienced before."

"I am happy they enjoyed it."

"You are ready."

"Ready for what?"

"To receive your spiritual name."

"I am?"

"Yes, Lakshmi Devi Ma. Lakshmi from Goddess Lakshmi, the goddess of wealth and good fortune. You will be this for the masses. You will help others to find their true self and have abundant lives. Devi means goddess and Ma means mother."

"Wow, thank you Nala."

"You can use your name as part of your practice."

"Oh, I am not sure I am ready for that."

"You'll know when you are so no rush."

We give each other a hug and begin dancing with the others.

38
The Enslaved

I am at the bookstore awaiting my turn to read from my second novel. This is my third book and second time reading at this event. The time before I read from the first book in my novel series and Cleo and Sophie's picture book. Mary said it was the first ever to have an author publish two books in under one year.

As I listen to the other authors read, I reflect on my dream with Diana Ross. She said everything I wanted would happen in one to two years. She was right in ways I didn't understand at the time. It's been almost three years since that dream. I thought she meant I'd be an overnight success living in my Malibu mansion but what she meant was everything I needed to live out my soul's mission would be discovered and it has. My meditation practice has deeply connected me to my soul where all the answers lie. This reconnection with my soul has also helped increase my self-love and strengthen my Solar Plexus. These years with Lucas has allowed me to experience love and know what I desire in a relationship and also know when it's time to accept the lessons and let go.

I hear my name announced by Mary. I stand and walk to the podium. I see Lucas in the audience beaming with pride. I read the prologue from my novel and just like before the room is in awe. I believe it's because I relate my experience to that of slavery. It's a relatable description for many regardless of race.

As the audience applause and I take my seat I feel my own sense of enslavement. I am writing this novel series to share my journey knowing it will help others and in doing so it allows me to see where I might be falling into another enslavement. While I am slowly breaking my way out of Shawshank, I have been slowly building another prison of sorts and that is my life with Lucas. I concluded in Ecuador that our relationship needs to end. I've been back just a few days and this is our first time together since my return. I see it so clearly this evening. Lucas loves me and he loves this side of me the most. The multibillion-dollar manager of the Air Force's budget and the self-published author who is unbashful in telling the truth about the Pentagon. This is who he loves and honestly it doesn't match up to the Ava now Lakshmi Devi Ma healer and lover of all.

How can I talk about racism at the Pentagon one minute and then give Reiki to a multicultural group at a meditation retreat? For me it's an easy answer. I love everyone and I want everyone to find their soul's purpose and freedom. And I will always love my blackness and my people just a little bit more. How could I not? For Lucas he is okay with me loving everyone just not supporting them with alternative healing methods.

The thing that is most curious is that Lucas seems to think we are just fine. It's like as long as he believes he will convince me to not discuss my work as a healer at least amongst his friends and colleagues then we are good. For me this is another Shawshank and something I cannot agree to do.

I see Lucas making his way to me.

"Congratulations, you blew everyone away. I love that part where you said how some of us are like the slaves who didn't escape with Harriett Tubman. How we are fearful of the unknown."

"Thanks. I think that's all of us at some point in our lives and sadly how some of us are for our entire lives."

"Well, we know that's definitely not you. I see there are some folks wanting to speak with you so I'll let you mingle."

"Thanks."

Lucas gives me a kiss on the cheek and walks off to mingle with the other authors and audience members. I smile as two women approach me with my book.

"What you said is my life. You captured my feelings of being trapped in my life so beautifully."

"Thank you. It was my existence for such a long time. I hope my books can help others to see they can free themselves."

"They will and they already have for us. Would you mind signing them?"

"I'd love to and thank you for your support."

I move to one of the nearby tables and sign the books with the pen I was using as a bookmark. As I hand the books to the ladies, I see Lucas approaching.

"I just had to tell you that you are the talk of this event. Everyone loves you!"

"Aw thank you!"

I glance around and see my stack of books has reduced to just two copies. While the others haven't spoken to me, I can see there is an interest in my work. I spot Mary and excuse myself from Lucas. I make my way to her and thank her for her support. As I make my way back to Lucas a few folks stop me and we chat. I sign a few more books and then unite with Lucas.

"I think I'm ready to head out."

"Are you sure?"

"Yes, I'm ready."

We walk out to Lucas' car and as he opens my door I give him a faint smile. I wanted us to have a fond memory of our last day together and this has been that day.

"Lucas."

"I don't want to hear what you're going to say."

"You know."

"Yes, I know. I've been watching you grow for nearly three years and it's been incredible. You don't fit any mold Ava. It's like you say in your books we are institutionalized. Some of us know it and want out, some of us know it and are happiest this way. And some of us don't know yet but know something's not right and they are the ones who struggle the most. I love my profession and it comes with being part of an institution."

"Wow, funny how I am just realizing that you are part of an institution."

"I am and I am okay with it. I am never going to be one of those doctors who travels the world providing my services to the unfortunate but you, well I have no idea of what you will do. Maybe move to Ecuador, maybe become a famous author and live in a beach house like you talk about or maybe you'll travel the world teaching others how to free themselves.

"I really thought you wanted me to conform to your ways."

"I did until this evening. The passage you read opened my eyes to your truth. I kept trying to convince myself that you and I are similar. I want to keep you in your institution where I am most comfortable with you but that is not where you belong."

"I've grown so much with you. We were meant to connect."

"We were and I have grown as well. I'm sure it may not seem like it but please know I am aware that I choose to stay in the safe zone and I am excited to see you fly."

Lucas kisses me gently on my lips and we hug. The drive back to my place was quiet and peaceful. He came inside to say goodbye to the girls. We will miss him but I know this is the right decision.

Now I see the hardness I was starting to feel from Lucas was his unwillingness or perhaps his inability to free himself. I understand and I get it. Not everyone is fighting to free themselves from something even if they know life would be so much sweeter for them.

39
My Girls

Cleo and Sophie are sitting on the exam table and I am standing next to them stroking their backs. We are waiting for the vet to give us the results of their blood work. Both of my babies have been sick for the past couple of days, vomiting with no appetite and Sophie is falling when she walks.

The door opens and the vet walks in. Her face is grim though she tries to look optimistic. It's 6 PM and we are one of the last patients here. I can tell it's been a stressful day for her as her blonde hair is coming undone from its bun and she looks as though she could collapse.

"Ms. McClure. There is no easy way to say this. Cleo and Sophie have kidney disease."

"What does that mean?"

She proceeds to explain and I listen intently. I need to know what to do to get them well.

"At this stage we can give them subcutaneous fluids to support them. This along with the medications and supplements will help get their appetites back though I want to be honest with you as there is no cure for kidney disease. At some point we will have to come to a decision about when to say goodbye."

There is a knot in my throat that is fiercely choking me. I knew this day would come and I am not ready for it in the least and not like this. They were supposed to transition because of old age, not with this and not because of a dog food recall that caused this disease. They are 16 and 13 and I know these are the ages when many toy poodles and Yorkies come to the end of their physical lives but they are all I have.

These little loves have been with me from Oklahoma to Virginia to California and back and many trips down south over the years. They have seen the majority of the men in my life come and go to include saying their goodbyes to Lucas a couple of months ago.

How can I be so spiritual and yet be in this much grief? I have learned so much about the soul and I understand more about the infinite beauty that comes with a soul free of its physical body. I see now how this was the message I received in my dream the other night. I was walking with Cleo and Sophie on top of a mountain. I looked up at the sky for a moment and when I looked back Cleo was on a swing in a tree. She was swinging back and forth over my head in a serene delight. Sophie was part of the sky. I couldn't see her I just knew she was everywhere. I woke up knowing they were telling me they would be leaving me soon and now here we are getting the message again from the vet.

I managed to get the girls in the car before breaking down and crying. I just can't see my life without them. They are the only living beings who have been a constant in my life all these years. I had hoped they'd make it into the Guinness Book of World Records as the oldest living dogs but this will not be the case.

It is not lost on me that Lucas is no longer in my life and he would have been so supportive. I do understand that was part of the perfect timing. I need to go through this alone. I need to feel this pain, grief and guilt and I need to heal from it. I know it's part of something bigger that I am here to help others with and as much as I want the girls and I to magically escape to a land where we live forever, I have to stand through this. Just like I had to accept it wasn't time to stay in California I have to accept this truth and I have to move through this pain.

40
Stuck in a Jeep

I didn't think my life could get any lower than finding out my babies will be leaving me soon but I am discovering in this very moment there may be another level of low for me. I believe this to be true because I can't get out of my Jeep.

I've made it to the parking lot of one of Shawshank's offsite locations in Fairfax County and I've been sitting here for about five minutes. I open the door. It's 40 degrees outside and I'm letting cold air sweep into the Jeep and across my bear legs. I am wearing knee-high boots and a skirt but no stockings. I'm moved by the chill but I still can't get out so I close the door.

I'll say another prayer and then I'll try to get out one more time.

"I love you God. Please help me get out of this Jeep. I think you've made it so unbearable I have no choice but to move; no choice but to follow my heart. To hell with how much I still owe for that fellowship. I have saved well over the years. I'll be okay. Please let me get out of this Jeep, go to this meeting and then make plans to move back to LA. I'll find any job in LA to supplement my savings and get back to my circle of LA people and my writing workshops. Southern California is my muse. Amen."

Though as I say this prayer there is loneliness in my heart. How can I return to LA without the girls? And I know I can't take them to LA now. They are dying. They were diagnosed a few months ago and while we've been doing daily vet visits for the subcutaneous fluids, and I've been making homemade meals and giving them supplements they are not getting any better as the vet explained the day I got their test results. They are simply not in pain and continue to live for me.

That's what the receptionist said at the holistic center they also go to for acupuncture and laser therapy. She said it must be the healing energy that she feels from me that is keeping them alive because their levels indicate that they should have already transitioned. Yet they are lively, in no pain and eating well. My love for them is keeping them here and I know I need to let them go.

I've been thinking about the losses in my life, Dan, Lucas and now the girls. I wanted Dan to be something that he told me upfront he couldn't be then I made it seem like he was the one with the problems. I was able to let Lucas go and he wanted a life with me but it wasn't a life I desired. And then there's my family. Over the years I've been less of a presence in my family and friends' lives. This was clear to me when my uncle thanked me for coming to my grandmother's funeral like I was some random attendee.

This was just last month. I arrived just in time, flying into the small Alabama country town in my rental car like a bat out of hell trying to make up for lost time as my connecting flight in Atlanta was delayed. I parked, hopped out and hurried across the patchy gravel parking lot to the front of the church. My uncles were greeting guests as they entered into the church. One was excited to introduce me as the niece that works at the Pentagon. The other thanked me for coming.

I recall sitting at the back of the church not with my family but in the last pew as I had gone to check on my mom who doesn't do funerals and was waiting for everyone to attend the repass in the basement. By the time I got back to the church's front entry the service had started and I slipped in quietly and sat at the back. It was here I knew I was a stranger to my family and my uncle was spot on to thank me for coming. I had debated making the trip down as I didn't want to leave the girls not even for one night as our time together is so precious. I do care more about them than my family and that is something my family has known for years. They seem to accept it well enough, I guess. I think they know just like I do that Cleo and Sophie are all I've had over the years and our bond is unbreakable. Even after they transition, I know we will remain close soul to soul.

"I've digressed again God but as I was asking, please give me the strength to leave this Jeep and the DMV. Cleo and Sophie leaving me feels like a sign it's time to leave the DMV again."

I look at the clock on the dashboard and see I am late for the meeting. I pick up my latte and take a sip. I know the answers are here. They are in me and I am allowing them to fester within me instead of fully acknowledging them. Okay, truth. I hate what I'm doing. I always have and that is not going to change. The more I ascend in my spiritual journey the more this career eats at me. War and destruction for the goal of U.S. and international peace is not my thing. Peace for the sake of peace is. Inner peace is the key to reconnecting with your soul and discovering your purpose for being on this earth, yeah that's my lane.

"Okay God. New prayer. Please help me say goodbye to my babies and help me to embrace your message to me which is to get the hell away from Shawshank as soon as possible regardless of if I still owe money back for that fellowship. Thank you, amen."

I put my seatbelt on and drive off. No one is going to care if I don't show up for this meeting. The truth is I could keep working here for another decade and then retire because this work is not hard but I say it with a forked tongue it is hard in that it's killing my soul.

Today is January 20, 2020, and today I am fully open to receiving the answers my soul has been waiting to give me all these years.

<h1 style="text-align:center">41</h1>
<h1 style="text-align:center">A Domino of Goodbyes</h1>

I woke up this morning feeling nauseous. I called in sick and continued to snuggle with Cleo and Sophie. They will be leaving me today. I know this because I just know. The same way I knew my grandmother was ready to go.

She gave me the tightest hug in my dream. I woke up and knew she was saying goodbye. I then spent the next several hours talking to her soul to soul. I told her it was okay to go. We would miss her but she was free to go. I told her we loved her, she had done so much for us, and she deserved to transition. Throughout the day I heard my grandfather telling me to tell her to hurry up. I laughed and thought about the day he transitioned. I woke up smelling his cologne. It was as if someone had saturated my bedroom with it. About an hour later my dad called to tell me my grandfather, his father-in-law had passed away.

I was driving the girls to the vet for their fluids and started crying uncontrollably. I kept saying I love you Madea and I miss you. I could barely see the road for my tears but somehow managed to arrive at the vet. Once we were inside the receptionist asked if I was okay. I told her, "I think I just helped my grandmother die."

"Oh, yeah that can be heavy."

This may seem like a strange response but she is one of the ones who gets it so there was nothing more to say. About an hour later I am driving home with the girls and my sister calls to tell me Madea has died.

"Yeah, I know."

"Who called you?"

"No one."

"Right. You know, you should do something with that gift or whatever it is you have."

"Yep, I should."

What was fascinating to me was the exact time that she died. My sister said she died at 5:31 PM Central Standard Time and at 6:31 Eastern Standard Time I was bawling my eyes out. I literally was right there with her when she transitioned.

It is now 4:25 PM and I have been in bed with the girls all day. They want nothing, no food, no potty breaks. I pick them up and lay them on my chest as they are so tiny they easily fit. Sophie is the first to take her final breath. I don't move. I continue to hold them both close to me. Cleo lets out her final breath and I feel the tears streaming down my face.

I slowly move them to either side of me and continue to lie on the bed. I need to take them to the vet and I will but I just need to rest for a bit. These last few months have been hard on us. Daily trips to the vet, the aching in my heart that wanted to hold on to them for dear life and the start of a pandemic. They have been such wonderful troopers and I thank them.

I lean over and kiss them then slide off the bed. I go to the closet to get their travel crate and come back to the bedroom. I gently place

Sophie inside and then Cleo. I close the door of the crate and look for my phone. I call the vet and inform them I will be arriving with the girls and the receptionist is in tears.

"They were the sweetest duo. I am so sorry for your loss."

"Indeed, they were, thank you."

I am leaving the vet deflated. This is my first experience with loss. I know I've lost all four of my grandparents but it's safe to say I love Cleo and Sophie more than them. Simple math shows this. I was with my girls every day with the exception of a short vacation or TDY for 16 and 13 years. I saw my grandparents throughout my fortysomething years of life twice a year for a few days at a time. There simply is no comparison.

42

COVID-19

Losing the girls at the start of this pandemic was hard and things at work are not making my life better. Maj Gen Deeds tagged me for a special COVID-19 safety campaign and being back in his orbit along with this depression from losing the girls and the daily death count I report for this project has helped me to see it's time to go.

I am one year short of my five-year payback for the fellowship and I just don't care. I found out that if I explain my emotional distress I may not have to pay back the remaining $12,000.00. I am working with our HR team and feeling really good about the outcome. I wrote a note in my phone and screenshot it for my unlock and wallpaper so I see throughout the day "I owe nothing and I am free."

As for my alternative healing business, my clientele has increased substantially. This pandemic has everyone on edge. My people and animal clients are seeking support for peace. Many of my clients are awakening to their truth which is they are not happy with some or all parts of their lives. They are a reflection of me. Before I heard my Spirit Team tell me to work with HR I was feeling like a fraud. How could I advise them on quitting their jobs when I was doing this as my side hustle? How could I when I knew God had made it very clear it was time to leave – when I was crying as I drove to work each day. Then the answer came and I took it and ran. I never thought I'd be one of those people who found what I would have considered a dishonest way to leave. But I now see those people differently and I understand.

Had it not been for the COVID-19 task force I would have been okay to complete my last year but reporting the daily death tolls and the constant reminder that we all have a limited time in these physical bodies was sending me into a massive depressive state.

People are dying of this COVID thing and while I believe I will be here for many more decades, I know I am wasting time and not fulfilling my mission. Through my meditation and other practices, I have cultivated a level of assurance. This place of confidence feels surreal. Was it not just a few years ago I sat in Dr. Smith's office week after week coming to the same conclusion about my life? I knew it was time to live for me and yet sometimes mere moments after leaving her office I was right back to that very low dark place.

I see now it wasn't just how my parents treated me. It was also the darkness of Shawshank that added to my self-imposed inertia. You take someone like me with a host of childhood trauma and place her into an abyss of dark energy and she's helpless. She is helpless until she has her awakening ironically afforded to her by Shawshank. But it all had to happen. It's just as I understood it during my hypnosis session with Amy only now, I truly get it. I know I will continue to heal and grow as I continue to support others as a vessel of healing and I am okay with that. I have to be as there isn't another way. I am human and I am also a divine co-creator of my life. And so it is.

43
Coco

A few weeks ago, I was walking into the veterinary center to see an animal client when I heard, "You will have a new dog in your family." I chuckled and thought sure thing God! All of these wonderful dogs I see here at the center are my extended family. Exactly 24 hours later I received a text from a neighbor asking me if I would like a dog.

I couldn't stop staring at the photo as she looked so much like my Yorkie Sophie. My heart was melting as I felt the tears flowing. The poor baby looked so sad and lost. She looked like I'd felt the majority of my life. Though I felt bad for her I knew having a dog was not ideal as the plans I was making had me relocating to Panama. I'd done quite a bit of research and was convinced that this was the right decision for me. Warm weather, mostly sunny days, affordable living and of course the water. And I could see my clients virtually and of course I could write from anywhere. It wasn't Malibu but it was away from the DMV. Malibu would come when my work as an author and healer gained more traction.

I resisted for days and tried my best to find someone I knew to take Coco. Finally, I decided to get her and try to rehome her while she stayed with me. My logic in this was that she just needed some extra loving and of course I was projecting my abandonment issues onto this poor puppy. As soon as we got home, she was at home. It was as though she'd been living here for the entire 8 months of her life.

When I went to my Zen room to meditate, she hopped on the daybed curled up on my lap and didn't move until I was done.

I understand our animals choose us and so this didn't surprise me as much as I was surprised how hard I was fighting it. Coco is here to keep me in the DMV because while it is time to say goodbye to Shawshank, I am not done in this area. God told me this some time ago and while I haven't forgotten this, I know sometimes I'm hoping I've fulfilled whatever it is. There was a time when I thought it was teaching many of my practices to my co-workers. Initially I thought it was because I was to meet Lucas. Other times I just knew it was so I could be a vessel of healing for the clients I have connected with but deep down I know while all these are part of it, they are not the whole.

Could I take Coco to Panama? Of course, I could but I don't want to go through the process of getting her cleared to enter the country plus I just know there something else I must experience here in the DMV.

For now, my little girl and I are happy right here. She is the spokesdog for my animal Reiki practice and she is my Anahata, my Heart Chakra. This baby is a bundle of love and while I am mindful not to become co-dependent as I did with Cleo and Sophie she has stolen my heart. She's super intuitive and my mini-me as animals are a reflection of their parents. She often brings me toys that express her messages for me. When I am having a moment of uncertainty, she brings me her Wonder Woman toy reminding me that my faith and strength will guide me. When I was unsure if the latte, I'd had for breakfast was upsetting my stomach she ran to her toybox and retrieved her puppuccino toy letting me know indeed it was. This might be unimpressive to some but since I've never taught her the names of her toys the fact that she knows what they are is fascinating.

We take walks along Mount Vernon Trail just like Cleo, Sophie and I did. We share snacks of berries and carrots and sit on the bank of the Potomac and just be. And Cleo and Sophie are there too. I feel their souls with us and the four of us are at peace.

44
Bathtub Reflections

Some of my spiritual downloads come when I'm soaking in the tub.

I deserve to live the life God placed me on this earth to live during this lifetime.

Southern California was my muse.

I attracted men who saw no value in me as I saw none in myself-you attract what you put out.

Months before I met Lucas, I prayed and asked God to open my heart, soul and mind to giving and receiving love. I was ready to start the journey and understand Lucas was not the destination but an amazing stop along the way.

I need to stay focused on the fact I came back this lifetime to be a successful author-to educate, inspire and entertain the world and it must be done. I don't have a choice to not make it happen as this is what I agreed to do with God before arriving on this earth as Ava McClure. It is my soul contract.

My clients are reflections of me. Some are a reflection of my past; some are a reflection of where I am today and some are foreshadowing my future. In all cases, I am able to support them because I have either the experience to share or I channel messages that serve to support their healing journey and mine.

Reflecting on Dan. Two broken people continuously hurting each other and breaking each other down even further not realizing there's a better way. I wanted a relationship with him because I had extremely low self-esteem due to a fucked up childhood and he in many ways matched the energy of what I was familiar with - disfunction. I will continue to be gentle with myself as I heal from my childhood trauma. There is always another layer of healing.

The other week I was visiting a new client for a house cleansing and Reiki session. Her apartment building was across the street from Dan's condo. I didn't think much of it when I went in to see her but after her session as I was leaving her building, I stopped and looked at Dan's building and smiled. I am in such a better place than I was just a few years ago. There were many evenings I discussed my dysfunctional relationship with Dr. Smith only to end up in Dan's bed the same night. Now here I am serving as a Reiki Master, a vessel of healing for someone else. Yes, we can all heal and move forward. We just have to want to do the work to make it happen.

Whether they did so intentionally or not my parents completely fucked up any chance I had of going into my adult hood with any sense of self love or self-respect. I can imagine though that it really wasn't intentional but just the same I am the one responsible for healing and moving forward with my life.

The few times I've seen Dan when he's at Shawshank for his reserve duty have been uneventful. We smile and keep walking. At first, I wished we'd had more closure but the more I heal and serve as a vessel of healing for others the more I feel the closure between us in an energetic way.

Although I was unhappy towards the end of my relationship with Lucas, I did hold on a bit longer because there were lessons to be learned. On the surface I believed it was because I'd never had such a soulful connection and didn't want to let it go but now, I understand that soulful connection was to make me stay in it for as long as I did to learn and grow. If I didn't have such a deep connection with him, I would've walked away sooner and I would've missed the many lessons.

My vibrator is loud. I'm sure my neighbors can hear it and I don't care.

If the military folks can wear BDUs (battle dress uniform) most or all days of the week, why can't civilians and contractors wear jeans and t-shirts?

I have an incredible attraction to extremely dark-skinned men. This reflection makes me chuckle as Dan was extremely fair skinned and Lucas was an Argentinian with blonde hair and blue eyes. I have not yet met my super hunky dark chocolate brother but I know it will be soon.

Not getting out of the Jeep that day was a pivotal moment. It was in essence the end of my federal career.

I fell in love with California because it transformed me; it opened me up, it broke me open and started the next part of my journey. Nala and Mona were there. The ocean was there. My ability to ground at Palisades Park was there. The girls and I regressed in age there. There were lessons learned after returning here. Amy is here and with her as my teacher I have evolved tremendously.

I wouldn't have the content to write a novel series about Shawshank had I not had this career. Returning to Shawshank has definitely helped shape my novels.

The soul knows what the soul needs and once you give it a taste of the good stuff- Reiki, meditation, crystals etc. it will never settle for anything less.

Only my soul fully knows what I've been through and what I've experienced and what it is I will capture in this lifetime to bring into the next. I am blessed that God allows me to have glimpses and understanding of my past lives and it's just enough to move forward and continue on my path. Equally I am blessed to have glimpses of my future and understanding of my purpose. Everything reveals itself at the right time.

Perception is everything. While my life hasn't been so awful compared to many other people's walks of life, it was awful for me in what I perceived was hurt, pain and neglect. Regardless of how others in my life view things, I am going to live my life the way I need to and no one can understand that but me.

It's not just about reading the books or **gleaning something from an Iyanla: Fix My Life episode.** It's about drilling in and doing the work. It's about **seeking help.** Maybe it's just a friend, maybe it's a pastor, maybe it's a Reiki Master, **maybe it is a counselor or therapist.** Maybe it's just reading the fucking book and really doing the work but whatever it is it's got to be done - **the work it must be done.**

I'm not good enough. This idea was placed in my head by the people who gave me physical life but it is not from God, it is not how I am looked at by the Universe. I am worthy, I am more than enough

I deserve all of my heart's desires. They were given to me before I was created as life for this worldly experience. I will see them manifest.

God will send others who will aid in helping me obtain my desires. I don't have to do all the work. I can stay open and receive.

I was in a codependent relationship with Cleo and Sophie or better yet a dependent relationship as I think they were perfectly fine and I was the one in need of them. I also placed myself as a low priority. I am thinking about some of the things I used to do that now clearly see was lack of love for myself. I used to put lavender behind Cleo and Sophie's ears and I'd have a little bit left over so I'd rub it on me. There were times when I'd make them a special dinner like chicken with rice and spinach and because it looked so good and they weren't going to eat it all I'd make myself a plate which was an upgrade to the takeout I usually ate for dinner.

My Dysfunctional Love Affair with the Pentagon is coming to an end. As this chapter of my life is closing, I am beginning to see it's been a blessing to have been back in the building. I feel what everyone feels who return – why the military come back after they retire as federal employees or contractors (the double dippers); for the money yes and for the familiarity. It's like staying in a bad marriage or someone who keeps coming home for the holidays to a dysfunctional family. You have better options staying home and ordering Chinese but yet you, book the flight, endure the crazy and then you wonder why. It's what you know and it's comfortable. I get that and I also get that this is part of my mission – to help people escape these mental plantations they've placed themselves on.

As I sit in this scalding hot bath, I realize I was bathing in the institutionalization of Shawshank and damn near drowned in it.

Most people are institutionalized - a little bit or perhaps a lot. It was clear to me that I had to escape but I too am institutionalized even without this device working, even in fulltime right brain mode it's ingrained in me. Every part of my life was steeped in institutionalization, drill sergeant father, school, college, Shawshank. Even Lucas pointed out hospitals are an institution. Basically, we were all raised as institutionalized slaves.

I am Red with the heart of Andy. I'm the institutionalized one. I know nothing but bureaucratic bullshit. I know nothing but getting things done. I know nothing but getting things done two, three and four times over - the same thing over again with a new project name. I once joked with the young captain at Big Brains and told him when he got his assignment at the Pentagon to look for Brooks, Red and Andy as every office has them. The Brooks's - you know the person that just retired and people still talk about them and tell funny stories about them. Occasionally someone says they saw them out and about in town. The Red's. They are those hard-pressed people working to get the job done. They know everyone in the building and at the MAJCOMs (major commands). They can pick up the phone and call anyone to get anything they need to get a tasker complete. The Andy's. The brand new majors and lieutenant colonels. It's their first time in the building - fresh out of the cockpit. They are jonesing to return to flying. I saw them so clearly. I could pick them out in every office and I just knew I was Andy but I'll be damn if I wasn't Red daydreaming of being Andy.

Since my return from Santa Monica, I've been more in Andy mode trying to escape. I knew if I didn't escape, I would Brooks myself from the inside. I would be at Shawshank with no hopes of having any type of life and that would be my mental death. I once had a supervisor say that you have to have a plan when you retire. What would my plan be if I waited until I was the minimum age of 57 to retire? I think I'd be so beaten down by the bureaucratic bullshit that I wouldn't have the drive to write. I'd just be some mentally drained human dragging myself out of Shawshank with a retirement certificate.

I chipped away daily, like Andy, only I did it by writing and starting my alternative healing business. I wrote what the Hollywood executives told me to write. I did not allow myself to get sucked up in this place. I did it. I freed myself. Thank you, Ms. Sally. And now I will be the modern-day Harriett Tubman. I will help others free themselves from their mental plantations.

45
Goodbye to Shawshank

I'm saddened. I'm almost numb and I'm at peace aware that leaving this place is a separation from my home and my family. Today I don't see Shawshank. Today I see my life and where a lot of changes and growth occurred as I look over this courtyard and see where Dan and I met.

I see people who get it, the Groundhog Day'ness who are not taking their yard break but rest for the next round before crazy. They are just being. I bet these are the ones who have great work life balance. I've been seeing them wrong all this time. And now I am them one week before I leave, one week before the unknown but it's the only way to continue to grow. Or, maybe they are disgruntled and this is indeed their yard break. Heck, I don't know their stories but today I choose to see them this way. And those sexy pilots in their flight suits, yeah, I'll miss seeing them too.

I am grateful to have had this career because it allowed me to tell the story of our Pentagon existence. Sure, we all see this place differently but I know my story will capture a lot of the emotions many feel.

I think though my sadness is more about change. It's knowing with every fiber of my being that I will never work in this building again. I am free of my servitude. It's as clear as I am a human. As steady as my faith in God.

I am wrapping up this book series at the same time I am wrapping up my time at Shawshank. There's meaning to this. Much like my Oprah dreams. We are always in a Starbucks and she's asking me if I've tried her chi tea latte and then she goes on to say how happy she is that it's doing well. I've been having this dream for five years and it never varies even though Starbucks no longer sells her chi tea latte. Of course it's bigger than the latte and now I understand it more than ever. I see it from her beginnings and where she is now. I see her not sticking to the safe way but making a way. I see her believing in herself and living her soul's purpose. She could still be a local television news personality but instead she's known around the world and lives out her soul's purpose. I can say without question now that yes Oprah, I'm drinking the chi tea latte and it taste delicious!

46
Reminder from My Soul

California had to happen; it's where you were broken open. Your return to the DMV had to happen; it's where you needed to begin healing your wounds and learn many new lessons.

You have lived a life with no love from those whom one would have thought would have been the ones to love and nurture you. They told you they didn't want you and while they never said the words, made it very clear they did not love you. They told you that you would fail, that you were not smart, that you were at best average and yet you excelled to places that they can't comprehend.

Your soul once lived in the body of a slave so you know you have been through worse. Your soul knew you were empowered to do and become much more and it wouldn't let you rest on mediocrity.

You didn't know then and didn't remember but your soul knew and it empowered you to forge ahead. You are just at the beginning of this life's journey and you will touch many lives with your love to give and serve others. You came into this world this time unwanted and unloved, neglected but for your basic needs of food, clothing and shelter.

You will rise higher than you can dream at this very moment and you will someday look back and smile more than you are smiling right now at how far you have come!

You have so much to give and you will continue to move forward and do so! You are here to educate, inspire and entertain the world through your writing! Your work as an Inner Peace Specialist will easily fold into your work!

Epilogue
Life as Lakshmi Devi Ma

There are days when my life feels surreal. Bestselling books, movie adaptation of *Illusions*, Cleo and Sophie's book now a cartoon series, hosting retreats around the world and giving inspirational talks to support others emancipate themselves. From turning in my badge just a few years ago to fully living in my soul's purpose in 2025 – what a blessing.

And I am loving life back on the West Coast! I have my eyes set on a neighborhood in Malibu and I know the right home will be for sale very soon. This neighborhood has been with me since I graduated from college. Over the years I've had many visions of driving through a neighborhood and pulling up to my beachfront home. A few months ago, my Spirit Team told me to drive up to Malibu from my home in Redondo Beach. I do my best to heed their guidance so I hopped in my Jeep with Coco and we set off for a leisurely drive up the PCH. After stopping and getting a latte, my Spirit Team told me to drive a little bit further and by this point we were deep into Malibu. Just when I thought we were about to leave Malibu I saw a sign noting beach access so I turned. To my surprise the street I turned on was the exact street I'd seen in my visions for 30 years.

I felt tears flow down my face as I knew this was home. It was 10 years ago that I was on the other side of LA county on Ventura Boulevard crying with sadness because I had to return to Shawshank. God's timing is always best. I fell in love with California in 2015 and was devastated when I had to leave in 2016. In 2024 God opened the door for me to return and continue my spiritual life coaching in Beverly Hills. Through my Spirit Team, He showed me my life here is just beginning as my neighborhood and new home awaits me. Everything has been right on time and it always is when we stay in faith.

I couldn't wait to share this news with Jay. Jayamma, whose name means praise the lord in Nigerian, and I met last year while Terry, Sheryl and I were enjoying a warm summer day at the Wharf in Southwest D.C.

Jay is patient, peaceful, strong in his faith, assured and steadfast. These characteristics are important to me because they reflect a person who has lived a life of ups and downs and has grown stronger from their experiences. He embraces all of life. Not every day is a great day but when you embody these characteristics every day will have peace and understanding. These qualities in him allow him to see me - the me that continues to heal as I serve as a vessel of healing for others. The me who continues to open up and embrace life as he does.

Others have seen my broken pieces and tried to manipulate me. Jay sees my broken pieces and supports my healing journey. He does this so lovingly because he's a man of God. God is in him and he too embraces his healing journey.

I am living my life with openness and peace. I embrace each moment and I get a lot of practice doing so since our relationship is long distance. For me this is a wonderful way to surrender to the present moment and let things flow as we continue to get to know each other.

Our love for each other is powerful. We are on equal footing – supporting and strengthening each other. Our strength is rooted in our connection to our ancestors; our understanding that we have a duty to rise to the greatest heights possible. Jay is of Nigerian and African American descent. He is the physical manifestation of the bridge we need to build between the continent and those of us who only know our lineage through slavery.

I feel the presence of our ancestors strongly with Ms. Sally's soul shining brightly as we lie on the beach here in Madagascar. I peer over at Jay through my sunglasses. I soak in his essence as I admire his dark brown skin glistening in the sun. I smile as I lean back in my chair letting the sun shower me with warmth and healing.